"I'm not making a mistake."

"You haven't spent an hour alone with him."

Lexi gave a mock eye roll. "Scout and I will get along just fine." She extended her hand to Heath. "Do we have a deal?"

Heath hesitated, then clasped her hand in his. "Deal."

"See? That wasn't so hard, was it?"

A smile tugged at his lips. "I'm most definitely getting the better end of this arrangement."

She tilted her head to one side. "Is that so?"

"One hundred percent." He pulled his hand away. "I've got to go."

Heath cut long strides across the yard toward his place. It didn't matter how sweet and generous his new neighbor was. She'd lost her husband. A horrific loss followed by the sorrow of carrying a baby alone. He knew a thing or two about horrific loss, and there was no way he'd start a relationship with someone who'd become a widow so young. Because more than likely, he'd make her a widow a second time.

Heidi McCahan is a Pacific Northwest girl at heart, but now resides in North Carolina with her husband and three boys. When she isn't writing inspirational romance novels, Heidi can usually be found reading a book, enjoying a cup of coffee and avoiding the laundry pile. She's also a huge fan of dark chocolate and her adorable goldendoodle, Finn. She enjoys connecting with readers, so please visit her website, heidimccahan.com.

Books by Heidi McCahan

Love Inspired

Home to Hearts Bay

An Alaskan Secret
The Twins' Alaskan Adventure
His Alaskan Redemption
Her Alaskan Companion

The Firefighter's Twins
Their Baby Blessing
An Unexpected Arrangement
The Bull Rider's Fresh Start

Love Inspired Trade

One Southern Summer

Visit the Author Profile page at LoveInspired.com for more titles.

Her Alaskan Companion

Heidi McCahan

LOVE INSPIRED
INSPIRATIONAL ROMANCE

LOVE INSPIRED®

INSPIRATIONAL ROMANCE

Recycling programs for this product may not exist in your area.

ISBN-13: 978-1-335-59680-2

Her Alaskan Companion

Copyright © 2023 by Heidi Blankenship

For questions and comments about the quality of this book, please contact us at CustomerService@Harlequin.com.

Love Inspired
22 Adelaide St. West, 41st Floor
Toronto, Ontario M5H 4E3, Canada
www.LoveInspired.com

Printed in U.S.A.

Fear thou not; for I am with thee:
be not dismayed; for I am thy God:
I will strengthen thee; yea, I will help thee;
yea, I will uphold thee with the right hand
of my righteousness.
—*Isaiah* 41:10

For Lisa Jordan. Thank you for being such a wonderful friend. This book was super fun to write thanks to our virtual writing sprints. I couldn't have finished this one without you.

Chapter One

Whoever said a dog was a man's best friend had never owned an animal like Scout.

Heath Donovan pried yet another dirty sock from his exuberant Goldendoodle's mouth. Scout promptly slathered Heath's forearm with slobbery kisses.

"You can't charm your way out of trouble. That doesn't work with me, dude."

Most of the time, anyway. As a police officer, he'd encountered plenty of hardheaded folks. Scout wasn't even a year old yet and he already excelled at being a repeat offender. Stealing socks, counter surfing, chasing squirrels like it was his job. Heath tried to maintain boundaries and implemented consistent training techniques. He'd watched a gazillion YouTube videos about positive reinforcement.

Then Scout would tip over the trash can in search of chicken scraps, Heath would admonish him and Scout would flop on his dog bed looking contrite.

Back to square one.

The mess and disobedience frustrated Heath to no end. But sometimes the mischievous furball was so stinking lovable that he couldn't possibly stay mad at him. When he sat on the sofa and watched TV, Scout often padded over, rested his snout on Heath's knees, and those big brown eyes melted away every ounce of irritation.

Heath tucked the sock out of reach on top of the refrigerator. "Come on, buddy. Let's go outside and burn some energy."

Scout pranced across the ash-brown laminate floor and Heath followed him.

Out in his backyard, the fragrance of fresh-cut grass greeted him. He'd mowed the lawn early this morning. After lunch he'd visit the hardware store and buy supplies to repair the damage that Scout had inflicted on the kitchen wall. Not that Heath had anyone to impress. He had no plans to invite people over because he preferred to be alone. That was why he'd moved to Hearts Bay. This rugged island community checked off all the right boxes. He could be self-sufficient. His job paid well and provided great benefits. And most importantly, he could keep his potential genetic disorder a secret.

A flash of white and brown captured his attention. Heath watched in awe as a bald eagle soared overhead. Add brilliant blue sky, lush green forests and incredible wildlife to his list of reasons why he liked living here. Scout trotted toward the bushes edging the back property line. Heath kept a careful eye on him. He'd made an appointment to have a contractor install a fence. That wouldn't be for another week, though. Thankfully, the Goldendoodle stayed close. Most of the time.

Scout looked back at him, tail wagging. Was he about

to run off? Heath braced for a sprint through the neighborhood.

"Scout, let's play." He grabbed a tennis ball from the bucket he kept by the back door. Scout's ears lifted slightly. One paw went up and curled. At least Heath had his attention. He chucked the ball across the grass. Scout took off, pink tongue lolling. His fluffy, coppery curls bounced as he loped toward the side of the yard. He pounced on the ball, then thrust his nose proudly in the air. The fuzzy tennis ball was clamped in his jaw.

Then he just stood there. Tail wagging.

Heath tapped his palm against his jeans. "Bring me the ball."

Scout stared at him, all four paws firmly rooted in place. This was maddening. What kind of dog with 50 percent retriever DNA refused to return the ball?

This ridiculous standoff happened often.

Heath sighed, then placed his hands on his hips. "Get a dog," his well-meaning friends had said back in Washington. "You need companionship. Having a pet is so rewarding."

Yeah, right, he thought, watching in dismay as Scout dropped the ball and flopped on the grass, rolling around on his back with all four legs extended in the air. Heath's mom and brother still lived in Spokane. Mom had not been thrilled about his decision to take this job with the Hearts Bay Police Force on Orca Island in Alaska. A state they'd only visited once when he and his brother were kids.

He had tried to explain to her that Spokane was great and he'd loved his childhood, minus the loss of his father, but he had to make a new start someplace else. Far from the people who'd known about his family's loss and all seemed to offer the same long, concerned looks dripping with empathy.

He refused to live that way.

"Scout, bring me the ball. Come on, boy."

The dog rolled to his feet but didn't return with the ball.

Movement from the corner of Heath's eye distracted him. He glanced next door. The house had been vacant when he had moved in six weeks ago. But recently, he'd noticed delivery trucks coming and going. Boxes and new appliances had disappeared inside the one-level rambler that, from the outside, looked much like his own.

However, this was the first time he'd seen evidence of the human who'd moved in. A woman crossed her back lawn carrying black plastic cartons of flowers. She looked to be about his age and wore white sneakers, navy blue leggings and an oversize navy-and-pink-striped shirt. Her dark brown hair spilled like a waterfall over her slender shoulders. She was singing softly. Pausing, she tipped her face to the sun and closed her eyes.

Heath couldn't look away.

He hadn't dated anyone in almost four years. His last girlfriend had wanted a diamond ring, a big wedding, the whole nine yards. *After* he did genetic testing to see if he had the markers for Huntington's.

Instead of giving her what she wanted, he'd ended the relationship. Because even though he didn't want to know if he could have the condition, he knew the odds were not in his favor. After that, he'd vowed to avoid romance and dating. No need to break someone's heart if he had a disease that would eventually kill him at a young age. Solitariness. That was his plan. His coping strategy. And he wasn't changing his mind.

Evidently some part of his brain had forgotten his intentions. Maybe he'd been too hard on Scout, because one glimpse at the beautiful lady who'd moved in next door and all logical thought vanished.

A four-legged blur of fur and lolling tongue dragged him back to reality.

"Scout. No!"

Ignoring Heath's command, the dog darted across the grass and hopped over the few pathetic shrubs that served as a property line. He had one destination in mind. Heath watched it all unfold in slow motion. Scout lunged at the woman, knocking the flowers from her hands.

She squealed and stumbled sideways.

Seizing the opportunity, Scout planted his paws on her hip and took her out. They tumbled to the grass. The woman was no match for his exuberant puppy energy. He proceeded to lick her face.

Heath shoved his hands through his close-cropped hair. "Oh, Scout. What have you done?"

Lexi Thomas lay flat on her back, staring at the clear blue sky overhead. A reddish-brown dog with a ginormous amount of curly hair licked her face. She'd always fancied herself a dog person. Two or three roamed through the peach orchard back home in Georgia. But this one had literally knocked her off her feet.

"Okay. Okay." A nervous laugh escaped her lips as she gently pushed the dog aside and sat up. His chocolate-brown eyes surveyed her face. He whined and sank down on his elbows, his hind end in the air and tail swaying like the sea oats outside her grandparents' beach house. Panting, his pink tongue spilled from his jaws, almost like he was offering her a toothy grin.

She rubbed her head. Oh, boy. Maybe she'd spent too much time alone, if she was giving this cute dog human characteristics. Maybe she'd addled her brain when she fell.

Her fingers found their way to the back of her head. Nothing hurt. No goose egg.

The baby.

Air whistled through her teeth. No harm could come to this precious child. He or she was all she had left of Beau. She pressed both palms to the cottony fabric over her abdomen. Falling wasn't great for pregnant women, right? She closed her eyes and mentally scrolled through the chapters she'd read in her book about preparing for pregnancy and a baby.

She'd meant to be more diligent about reading that book, but whenever she started, she promptly fell asleep.

"Ma'am, I am so sorry. Are you all right?"

She squinted into the sun, trying to identify the source of the deep voice. It was smooth, like syrup on a stack of hot pancakes, and belonged to a man. A tall, handsome man. He filled her frame of vision. Sandy-blond hair cut short with military precision. Tan, muscular arms peeked from the short sleeves of a brick red cotton T-shirt. His jeans were faded yet comfortable looking and he wore a popular brand of athletic sneakers.

"I'm fine. Just surprised is all."

Lexi let her eyes wander from his long legs, slim hips and broad shoulders to his gray-blue eyes. Deep crevices were etched on his otherwise perfect brow. *Okay, settle down. Beau's only been gone three months.*

Must be the pregnancy hormones wreaking more havoc.

Her hands traveled from her abdomen to her sternum. She pressed her palms against the sharp ache. Since her husband's sudden death in a military accident overseas, grief had been her nearly constant companion.

The man extended his hand. She hesitated, then took it. His grasp was warm and strong. Comforting. He took her other hand and gently pulled her to her feet. *Oh, my.* He smelled good. Like soap and pine trees and fresh air. *Stop.* She gave herself a mental shake.

He stepped back, then released her hands and gave her a polite, respectful once-over. "I'm so sorry about my dog."

"Apology accepted." She offered a reassuring smile. Poor guy. He looked mortified. "Your dog is quite friendly."

"And extremely disobedient." He glared at the animal. "Not cool, my man. This is no way to meet the new neighbor."

The dog yipped, then rolled over on his back. The universal canine sign for demanding a belly rub.

Lexi couldn't help but laugh.

The stranger scowled.

She smothered her laugh with her fingertips.

"I'm Heath Donovan."

"Lexi Thomas." She tugged free a strand of hair that had stuck to her lip gloss. "Nice to meet you."

"This is my wretched pet. Scout."

"Hey, Scout." She reached down and gave the dog a tender pat on his exposed chest.

Scout rolled to a stand, offered another friendly bark,

then promptly sat back on his haunches. He thumped his tail in a circular motion on the grass.

"Is he a poodle or a retriever?"

"A Goldendoodle. Also known as the biggest mistake I ever made."

"Yikes." Lexi grimaced. "Harsh words. Are you not a dog person?"

Heath palmed the back of his neck. "I'd prefer one who didn't knock people down and trample their flowers. I'll get you some more."

"It's all right. They're flowers. Easily replaceable."

Okay, so that wasn't exactly how she felt. While the flowers she'd purchased to fill the empty planters left behind by the previous owners hadn't cost much, her photography business was getting off to a slow start, and she didn't exactly have extra funds to waste. Her survivor benefits helped some, but she needed to find a way to earn more money. And soon. She had to be prepared to provide for her baby.

But her new neighbor looked so discouraged and put out with his dog that she downplayed the seriousness of the offense. That was what she always did. Smoothed things over. Infused sad feelings with inspirational thoughts, and did her best to make bleak circumstances feel hopeful.

"FYI, I've hired someone to build a fence. Probably be another couple of weeks until he has it installed and painted, though."

She rubbed her hands against her rounded stomach. "Thanks for the heads-up. I'm afraid I can't contribute financially. A fence isn't really in my budget…"

"No, this is on me." He crossed his arms over his muscular chest. "Scout is not great with boundaries."

She frowned. Maybe she should find a way to chip in a few hundred bucks. How much did a fence cost? Heath had Scout, but she was going to have a baby. Her child would need boundaries, too. Even though she wasn't due until December 12, surely her little one would be out here crawling by next summer.

It was all too overwhelming to think about.

"Are you sure you're okay?"

Heath hadn't come anywhere close to smiling since he'd shown up in her yard. He sounded genuinely concerned, though. Maybe Scout's behavior had put him in a bad mood.

"Yeah, just overwhelmed by everything that goes into owning a house. I'm also pregnant, which adds to my already lengthy to-do list. I was thinking maybe I'll need a fence, too."

All the color drained from his face. He shot a worried glance toward her house. "You're *pregnant*?"

"Don't worry." Her voice wavered. "No one's going to come out here and yell at you. I'm a single mom-to-be." And maybe not the first thing she should share with a stranger.

His gaze swung back to meet hers. He really did have mesmerizing eyes. Slate gray with specks of blue. Long eyelashes and a strong, masculine brow.

"I can't believe my dog knocked down a pregnant lady. Do I need to take you to the emergency room? Are you sure you don't need someone to look you over?"

She pressed her hand to his forearm. "Heath, I'm fine. I don't even know why I told you I'm expecting."

His eyes dipped to her fingers lingering on his arm. "H-how far along?"

She quickly pulled away. "Fifteen weeks."

Man, she was a mess. Shame twisted her insides. She'd recently buried her husband, and here she was, sizing up the new neighbor. Probably coming off super desperate.

Admiring Heath's handsome features had to be her hormones' fault. Granted, being a military wife wasn't easy, especially through multiple deployments, but she'd *always* been faithful to Beau. He'd bought this house for her when they'd visited Hearts Bay before he had shipped out again. Then an improvised explosive device had wrecked the future they'd dreamed of sharing. She wasn't ready to open her heart to love again. Not this soon. Maybe not ever.

He had to make this right.

Heath backed his truck into the driveway, climbed out and circled around to the tailgate. He hadn't thought to ask Lexi what kind of flowers she wanted. The ones scattered across the grass had been red. Or were they pink? He'd been so flustered. Not to mention embarrassed. And finding out she was pregnant had made the whole situation a thousand times worse.

Scout was out of control. Time to double down. That dog had to start consistently obeying the first time Heath gave a command. Before something more significant than flowers were damaged. He grabbed two bags of potting soil from his truck's bed and crossed the narrow strip of land that separated his property from Lexi's. The online training videos made compliance seem so easy to teach. A few of the tactics had helped some, but Scout's impulsiveness still ruled the day. When he got to Lexi's backyard, he set the potting soil on her patio and returned to the truck for the cartons of flowers.

When he rounded the corner of her house again, Lexi stood outside her back door.

"Hey," she said with a sweet grin.

Her smile made his pulse skitter. *Nope. Not going there. Romantic relationships are not an option. Remember?*

"I was in such a hurry to get you some new flowers that I left without asking what kind you wanted. I hope these are okay."

"They're gorgeous." She gestured toward the bags on the concrete. "You got potting soil, too. Thank you. How much do I owe you?"

"Nothing. I'm the one that owed *you*."

"Well, in any event, Scout is welcome to visit anytime." She held a clear reusable water bottle in one hand. Her fingernails were painted bright pink. He hadn't wanted to notice, but the shade matched the polish on her dainty toes.

"That's kind of you, but I'm going to keep him leashed or tethered to me when we're outside. He's a rascal."

"An adorable rascal." She spoke with the most intriguing Southern accent, then sipped her water.

He looked away, pretending to assess the planters that stood empty. "Where are you from?"

She hesitated.

"You don't have to answer that if you don't want to." He could relate to someone who didn't want to offer personal details about their past.

"It's complicated. I lived in Georgia. My late husband— Ooh." She fanned her fingers back and forth in front of her face. "I didn't know saying those words out loud would make me feel so emotional."

Could he disappear now? The sheen of moisture in her beautiful golden-brown eyes made him want to run back inside his house. Scout had already intruded on this woman's space. Now he was poking around in her business and making her cry.

"My husband, Beau, was stationed at Fort Benning. I grew up a few miles south of Macon, where my family owns peach orchards. Anyway, I found out I was born here. About thirty-six years ago. Somehow I was switched at birth with another baby."

Wow, this woman had been through a lot. "That is wild."

"Tell me about it! It took me forever to find my biological family, but when I did, I arranged a visit. That was over a year ago, and I loved Hearts Bay so much I wanted to move here."

"You're a brave woman."

"I don't know about that. My family back in Georgia is not happy. They stopped speaking to me when I came to the island to meet the Maddens. That's my birth family."

"You're estranged from the people who raised you?" His chest squeezed. He couldn't keep the judgment from his voice. "Please tell me they've changed their perspective now that you're—"

"A pregnant widow?" Lexi finished his sentence. She paused, then swallowed hard. "I keep praying that the Lord will soften their hardened hearts."

Her words landed like a gut punch. He didn't want to talk about the Lord. When God chose not to heal his father, Heath's faith had withered. He still believed

God existed; he just didn't trust Him to answer prayers anymore.

"Beau had some reservations about me coming to Alaska, but I'm glad he bought this house. This feels like the right time for a fresh start. Even though he's passed away and won't be here with me, I still wanted to live in Hearts Bay."

"This place is something special," Heath said. "I can't quite explain it."

"It's breathtaking. People keep telling me I'm in for it once winter arrives, and there's not much daylight. Evidently it rains a lot." She lifted one shoulder. "That's my story. How about you? Where are you from?"

He should've seen the questions coming. "I grew up in Spokane, Washington."

"Do you still have family there?"

His mouth went dry. He scrambled to find a new topic. Something safe. He didn't want to talk about his dad or Huntington's disease. He didn't really want to talk about family at all. However, Lexi's willingness to share personal details made him feel like he had to at least offer something. "I moved here for a new job. Like you, I thought Alaska sounded like a whole lot of fun. I've also been warned about the weather."

"So we'll both experience our first Alaskan winter together. That's exciting! I mean, not *together* together. As neighbors."

Pink blossomed on her cheeks. Normally he cringed when people tripped over their words. But Lexi made it seem…appealing.

She took another sip of her water, then pinned him with a curious look. "You said you moved here for work?"

"I'm a police officer."

"Oh, wow. That's cool. Do you enjoy it?"

"So far. I just started on June 1. We're staying busy." He shrugged. "Mostly traffic incidents and minor emergencies. Tourist season brings a lot of people to the island. How about you? Getting settled?"

"I've unpacked. Now I'm trying to come up with a long-term financial plan."

"How's that going?"

"Not great. I've been so exhausted and haven't devoted much time to getting my photography business up and running. I'm worried about how I'll make ends meet when I have a newborn baby."

"What if you sponsored a booth at Fish Fest and took pictures of families?"

She quirked a brow. "Fish Fest? What's that?"

"Hearts Bay's annual festival celebrating a successful fishing season."

"Oh, right. A lady at the coffee shop mentioned something about that."

"It's next month. Second weekend in August," he told her. "If you want to have a booth, you probably ought to sign up soon."

She nodded. "You're right. It sounds like a pretty big deal."

"There's a meeting later this week. I saw the announcement on a bulletin board at the station. Would you like more information?"

"Yes, please." She held out her palm. "If you give me your phone, I'll put my number in. Then you can text me."

Texting? Really? He stared at the ground, silently groaning. Couldn't he just bring her the flyer? He'd rather walk across hot coals than send a text. Hoping she hadn't sensed his hesitation, he pulled out his phone, unlocked it, then handed it over.

Her fingers flew across the screen. "There." She gave his phone back. "Now we're connected."

Her smile, paired with the whisper-soft touch of her fingers against his, captivated him. He was tempted to sit down in the Adirondack chair nearby and settle in for the afternoon.

"I—I'd better go. Scout's been in his crate so he doesn't destroy my place."

"Is that where he stays all day when you're at work?"

A wave of guilt gushed through him. "The breeder recommended crate training. It gives him boundaries and a routine. Which he certainly needs."

Drat. Now he was getting all defensive.

She quirked her mouth to one side. "I'm not a dog trainer, but I think Scout needs more one-on-one attention."

He frowned. She was probably right.

"I hope I haven't overstepped. How you care for your dog is none of my business. But if Scout needs a sitter while you're at work, I'd be happy to help."

"I can't ask you to do that."

A cute little divot formed in her smooth brow. "Why not?"

"You just moved in."

Her golden-brown eyes sparkled. "I'm unpacked. Now all I have to do is build a baby and find some clients."

Heath was not amused. Scout had knocked her down and ruined her flowers. Now she was offering to dog sit? Her kindness made him uneasy. Made him feel things he hadn't felt in a very long time. He gave those thoughts an impatient shove. "I'm not going to let you watch my dog for free."

"All right. What's the going rate for a dog sitter?"

"I have no idea." He'd meant to ask around. See if any high school kids offered pet-sitting services.

A plan took shape quickly. He was the guy who made a list of pros and cons. Talked to a few friends for advice, did online research before he decided. But Scout's behavior wasn't improving. He didn't have the luxury of a lengthy fact-finding mission.

"What if we made a trade?"

"What kind of trade?"

"If you watch Scout, I'll pay for the fence around your property as well."

She shook her head. "I'm not sure what a fence costs, but that does not seem like a fair trade."

He squeezed the back of his neck with his hand. "All right. Well, I'm a terrible cook, so I can't offer meals."

"Don't need any. My freezer is packed."

See? This was why he didn't make rash decisions. It only led him into uncertain territory. "Actually, on second thought, maybe this isn't a great idea after all."

"Why not?"

He shifted uncomfortably. "I'm concerned about how you'll safely take care of Scout as your pregnancy progresses. He's already jumped on you once. What if he knocks you down or gets loose and you have to chase him?"

She tapped a polished fingernail against her lips. "How about if I watch him for the rest of the summer? It's about six weeks until Labor Day, which gives you plenty of time to find and hire someone else. And in exchange for my stellar dog-sitting services, you'll help me do whatever I need to do for a booth at Fish Fest."

Heath studied her, silently calculating her terms. "You won't be in your third trimester yet?"

"Nope, not until October."

"And if Scout harms you or puts you or your baby in danger, you'll let me know immediately?"

"Absolutely."

He sighed, realizing there was no talking her out of this. "Okay…if you are sure. But if he drives you bananas and you realize you've made a huge mistake, you'll tell me?"

"I'm *not* making a mistake."

"You haven't spent an hour alone with him."

Lexi gave a mock eye roll. "Scout and I will get along just fine." She extended her hand. "Do we have a deal?"

He hesitated. Then he clasped her hand in his. "Deal."

"See? That wasn't so hard, was it?"

A smile tugged at his lips. "I'm most definitely getting the better end of this arrangement."

She tilted her head to one side. "Is that so?"

"One hundred percent." He pulled his hand away. "I've got to go."

Heath cut long strides across the yard toward his place. It didn't matter how sweet and generous his new neighbor was. She'd lost her husband. A horrific loss followed by the sorrow of carrying a baby alone. He knew a thing or two about loss, and there was no way he'd start a relationship with someone who'd become a widow so young. Because more than likely, if things progressed between them, he'd make her a widow a second time.

And that terrified him.

Chapter Two

Her bank account balance made her want to weep.

Lexi slumped against the tufted cushions of her green velvet sofa. Clutching her phone, she refreshed the screen, hoping somehow the app would offer a bigger number this time.

Nope.

She blew out a long breath and scrolled through her recent activity. Groceries, cleaning supplies, three frames for photos she'd hung on the walls and some newborn pajamas that were too cute to pass up. The military's survivor benefits had kept her afloat thus far. But she'd have to manage her money more carefully. The cost of living on an island was much higher than she'd anticipated. And based on everything she'd heard and read so far, babies were expensive.

Back in Georgia, she'd had no trouble finding new clients. But here in Hearts Bay, she'd photographed one event, and that was only because the Maddens hired her for Mia and Gus's wedding. Grief had been all-consuming in those first weeks after Beau died. She'd muddled through the funeral, packing up their belongings and arranging them for shipment to Orca Island. Then she'd stayed with the Maddens until her household goods had arrived on a barge last week. And since getting unpacked and settled had taken up so much of her free time, she hadn't made marketing her business a priority.

But that was to be expected, wasn't it? People kept telling her to take it easy. Even Beau had cautioned her to pace herself. Although he'd been overprotective as soon as she'd shown him the positive pregnancy test. The first trimester fatigue was no joke. Every time she sat down to brainstorm or design an ad for social media, the need to nap overwhelmed her. There was no way she had enough energy or stamina to make it through a session with a client.

Lexi closed out the app, tossed her phone on the sofa, then pressed her palms to her cheeks. She stared out the window into her backyard. Her *fenceless* backyard. Yesterday's conversation with Heath had left her feeling conflicted. Of all the things she'd have to buy in the next six months to prepare for a child, not to mention the diapers and wipes she'd need once the baby was here, a fence didn't rank high on the must-have list. The Maddens checked in often. This morning she'd casually asked her brother-in-law Asher how much he thought a fence might cost. He'd explained that everything cost more here because the materials had to be brought in by boat or plane. His best guess was about eighteen hundred dollars.

Yeah, not happening.

Heath had said his property would be fenced within the next couple of weeks. If only she could hire the same contractor to install a fence around her entire yard. The lot wasn't that large. But it was an ideal size for a dog. Or three. Her agreement with Heath had prompted her to brainstorm about dog sitting for other families in town. But she'd need to have a fence built first. And maybe give herself a week with Scout to see if pet sitting was something she could realistically handle.

One thing was for certain—she was *not* going to ask anyone to loan her money, especially not the Maddens. Her biological family had been so gracious to her already.

The postcard from Beau's parents sat propped against a white pillar candle on her modern coffee table. They'd saved up to take their dream vacation, a cross-country road trip in their RV. After Beau had passed away, Lexi had expected them to postpone. But they'd left their home in Indiana shortly after the funeral, and hoped to make it to Alaska before summer's end. An image of the Grand Canyon filled the front of the card. Her in-laws were in good health, but she didn't know them very well, and wasn't sure she'd be emotionally ready to meet them in Homer or Anchorage or wherever they parked their RV once they arrived.

She'd always be connected to them by their mutual love for Beau, and she carried their first grandchild. Beau's two sisters were still in their twenties and didn't have children yet. The note on the postcard from Beau's mother had mentioned a slight delay because their RV had broken down. The replacement part required a special order and hadn't arrived. Yet another reason she didn't want to call and ask for a loan.

Mainly, she just didn't want to ask for help. Plenty of people in her life had warned her that moving to

Alaska as a pregnant widow would be a huge mistake. Yet something about Hearts Bay and the island's rugged beauty had grabbed ahold of her. Even Beau had agreed, and he was the most risk-averse human she'd ever met. Her throat tightened. Wow, she missed him. Beau's sudden death had nearly flattened her. Sometimes thinking about all that was ahead, everything she'd have to face without him, made her want to crawl into bed and hide for days. Some small part of her still clung to the hope that she could be happy here. And now that she'd put all that time and energy into relocating, she wasn't about to pack up and leave again.

Besides, the naysayers back home would gloat for *years* if she tucked tail and ran home.

No matter how daunting the future seemed, she had to find a way to rebuild her life here. Hearts Bay had become a popular destination for weddings, because of the heart-shaped rocky outcropping off the coast. A hotel owner had built a beautiful new venue, but according to the Maddens, the brides all had photographers scheduled and hired already. Which unfortunately meant she had little hope of booking more weddings this year. People didn't exactly want to hire the new lady to shoot their big day when they could bring a reputable photographer in from Anchorage.

She wasn't giving up, though.

Thanks to Heath's suggestion and his willingness to help her get ready, a booth at Fish Fest next month would hopefully generate new leads. If twelve families booked holiday photo sessions, her account balance would get a nice boost. And she could stop worrying about finances.

At least for a few months.

A loud bark followed by claws tapping against glass pulled her from her deliberations. She turned and spotted Scout standing on the other side of her sliding glass door, a tennis ball wedged in his mouth and his tail wagging. Those chocolaty-brown eyes pleaded with her to come out and play. She could not resist.

Chuckling, she crossed to the slider, slipped on her flip-flops and opened the door.

"Hey, Scout." She stepped outside. "Do you want to play?"

He dropped the ball on the concrete at her feet with a *thunk-thunk-thunk* and stared at her expectantly.

She picked up the toy and gave it a half-hearted toss. He trotted across the grass and scooped up the ball before it stopped rolling.

Lexi slid the door shut. When she turned around, Scout had already brought the ball back. He dropped it at her feet again. Grimacing at the grass and slime clinging to the neon green fuzz, she chucked the ball a little farther this time. He gave chase immediately, brought it back and dropped it by her polished toes.

"Wow. You're really into this."

They repeated the cycle a few more times.

"No way." Heath strode toward her, shaking his head.

"What?" She hesitated, her arm half-cocked for another lob. "What did I do?"

Scout barked impatiently, his eyes locked on the tennis ball.

"You did nothing other than give him exactly what he wanted. He never brings that ball back for me three times in a row."

Lexi shrugged and threw the ball again. "I guess he just likes me more than you."

Oh! Had she *really* said that? She sucked in a breath.

The corners of Heath's mouth twitched. "I see how it is, Scout."

"I'm sorry, Heath." Warmth flushed her cheeks. "That was rude."

"Don't worry about it." He turned to face her. "I think you're probably right. Which is a good thing, since you'll be spending a lot of time together."

Lexi clapped her hands. "Am I still starting tomorrow? We should talk about your schedule, how often he eats, where you keep his favorite toys…"

"I was on my way over when Houdini here sneaked out and beat me to it." He gestured toward Scout. "My shift starts at eight a.m. tomorrow. I'm not off until five, and I work Tuesdays through Saturdays. I don't expect you to dog sit all that time, though. I'll drop off a house key tomorrow, if that works for you?"

"Or you can bring Scout over before you leave."

Heath frowned. "Full-time dog sitting is not what I had in mind."

She lifted one shoulder. "It's what I had in mind. If I need to go somewhere, I'll put him in your house in his crate. So I'll need a spare key."

"Thank you," Heath said. "You're being very generous."

"So are you. We haven't discussed what I'll need for Fish Fest."

"I hope I wasn't too bossy. I'm the last guy who should be handing out marketing advice to small-business owners."

"You weren't bossy. You offered a great suggestion. I'm not about to turn away from an opportunity to attract more customers." She stopped short of saying what was really on her mind. She was a widow and a single mom-to-be. There was no other choice but to be proactive. Her baby depended on her.

Donovan, what *are you doing?*

Heath traced the toe of his sneaker along a hairline crack in her patio. She'd mentioned feeling overwhelmed. Worried about money. Should he offer to help with any other repairs that came up?

Stop. He had no business standing here trying to make small talk. Or pretending he wasn't stalling. "So I'll bring Scout over around seven forty-five tomorrow morning. Is that okay?"

"Sounds good." She shivered, then rubbed her hands against her bare forearms. Visions of draping his jacket over her shoulders and pulling her close filtered through his head. Oh, brother. Yet another wild idea that could never become reality. But on the other hand…there was nothing wrong with neighbors looking out for each other.

Except he'd never lived next door to a human as lovely as Lexi.

After his last breakup, he'd declared friendships with single women off-limits. It was too painful. Not to mention unfair. He couldn't put his heart—or another person's—in jeopardy.

"If he doesn't eat before you bring him over, feel free to drop off a bag with his food." Lexi's voice tugged him back to the present. "I have bowls he can use."

"Right." He pulled out his phone and opened the notes app. "I'll make a short list of stuff he'll need and I'll be sure to bring it over."

This dog. Something told Heath he was going to get

the royal treatment while he stayed with Lexi. Scout looked up from exploring the base of a tall pine tree like it was the best thing he'd ever discovered. Why did he like Lexi's yard so much better than his own?

Heath quickly added a list of Scout's must-haves. Then he stole a peek at Lexi. She didn't seem annoyed that he and Scout had dropped by uninvited. She'd gathered her silky dark hair in a ponytail, revealing long dangly earrings that bounced against her slender neck whenever she moved. *Cute.* He forced himself to look away.

"I'd better get going." Pocketing his phone, he whistled for the dog. "Scout, let's go."

Scout's head poked up. He wagged his tail, then clamped a stick in his mouth. The branch was at least three feet long, and one end dragged across the grass as the pooch trotted toward them.

"What in the world?" Lexi laughed. "Where'd you find that?"

Heath groaned. "Scout, you are something else."

The dog dropped the partial tree on the cement patio and sank down on all fours.

"Nice work, Scout. I've been meaning to clean up that part of the yard." Lexi's bracelets on her wrist jangled as she reached down and patted Scout's head. He returned her affection with slobbery licks on her arm.

Oh, boy. The dog was smitten already. "C'mon, buddy. We've got to run some errands."

Much to his surprise, the dog stood, abandoned his stick and trotted toward their yard.

"How about that," Lexi mused. "He's already on his best behavior."

"It won't last." Heath stared after his dog in disbelief. "I'll see you tomorrow morning."

"See ya." She waggled her fingers and offered another smile.

Man, she was stunning. He stood rooted to her patio. His pulse thrummed. Scout's impatient bark echoed through the air, an obnoxious reminder of Heath's priorities.

He jogged toward his own back door, where the dog already stood waiting. "Let me get this straight. You visit her whenever you want. But when I want to stay and chat, you can't wait three extra seconds. What's up with that?"

Scout gave him a petulant full-body shake, then pawed at the glass.

"Why am I trying to carry on a conversation with you?" He shook his head, scoffing at his own inane behavior, then tugged the door open. Scout owned him already. How embarrassing.

Inside, the canine circled the kitchen island, panting.

"All right, all right. Patience, please." He filled the water bowl and set it on the floor. "There you go."

Scout pushed past him and lapped it up, flinging droplets of water all over the place.

Shaking his head, Heath pulled his phone from his pocket. It hummed in his hand. The word *MOM* and her familiar number appeared on the screen. He quickly answered. "Hello?"

"Hi, sweetie. How are you?"

"Fine. Mostly. Trying to plan for Scout to stay with my new neighbor."

"Does he have a dog boarding business?"

Hesitating, Heath dragged his fingers along his jaw.

Not that he'd ever lie to his mother, but if he told her about Lexi, he knew exactly what she'd say. And he didn't want to get her hopes up. "No, she does not. We've made a trade. I'm going to help her with a booth at the local festival next month and she's going to watch Scout for me."

"*Ohhhh*, I like where this is going!" She didn't even try to conceal her excitement. "I'm so glad you've met someone. And so soon. What's her name?"

He squeezed his eyes shut and stifled a groan. "No, Mom, it's not like that. We're neighbors and are both new here, so—"

"That's great. You can explore the island together."

"Please. Just stop. We've talked about this. I'm not interested in a relationship."

Her disappointed silence made regret pool in his stomach. Maybe he could've toned that down a bit.

"You sound like your brother, Reid," she said. "A delightful young woman just started as the new administrative assistant in our office. I've told Reid all about her, but he flat refuses to drop by and ask her out."

Smart man. Heath kept the comment to himself and picked up Scout's blue stuffed gorilla, tossing it across the room. The dog bounded after the toy, his nails clicking against the floor. He pounced, then flopped down, gnawing on the gorilla's ear.

Heath leaned against the counter and refocused on his conversation. Even though he anticipated more advice he didn't want to hear.

"You can't let your father's illness dictate your choices, honey. He wouldn't want that, and I don't want that, either. If you'd get genetic testing done, then you'd know more about—"

"That's the thing, Mom." He pushed away from the counter and paced the floor. "I don't want to know."

"But wouldn't it give you peace of mind? Depending on the results, you can plan for your future. Wouldn't that be better than having this cloud of uncertainty hovering over you all the time?"

He tipped back his head and glared at the ceiling. They'd had this conversation so many times. It was completely unproductive. He infused his voice with as much patience as he could muster. "Listen, I know how much it cost you to care for Dad. I hate that this cruel disease has stolen so much from our family, but I cannot ask a woman to commit to a relationship, knowing she might have to care for me. Or worse, care for me and be a single parent to our children after I'm gone. It's not right."

"I respect your decision, but I don't agree," his mom said quietly. "I'm going to pray that the Lord changes your heart."

"I appreciate your prayers." He stared out the living room window toward Lexi's house and half listened as Mom gave him the latest updates on her garden, friends from church and her plans for the evening.

His mother's comment about peace of mind bothered him. Meeting Lexi was making him question his life choices. He'd already done the research online, and genetic testing for Huntington's wasn't advised unless he developed symptoms. Which he hadn't. *Yet.* But that didn't mean it wasn't still a possibility. And he'd meant what he said. He couldn't put a woman through the horror his family had endured, watching Dad succumb to the disease. Which meant he'd have to work doubly hard to squelch his attraction toward Lexi. Sure, they'd established a convenient, mutually beneficial arrangement, but that was all it was.

And he'd be wise to remember that.

Lexi tucked the flyer about Fish Fest along with the notes she'd hastily scribbled on a scratch piece of paper inside her straw tote bag. Heath's advice about attending the information meeting for the upcoming festival had been super helpful. She'd have to text him a thank-you later. The week had flown by in a blur of taking care of Scout, brainstorming ways to find new photography clients and napping. She didn't want to admit it, but watching a rambunctious Goldendoodle had sapped her energy.

With her mind spooling through all the new information she'd absorbed, Lexi wove her way through the small clusters of people mingling in the Town Hall's conference room. She exchanged polite smiles and waved to three women who'd graciously brought her meals and had helped her unpack. Hearts Bay was full of friendly residents. They'd made her feel welcome, and the curious stares didn't bother her anymore. She'd visited over a year ago and attended the commemoration of the earthquake that had occurred the day she was born. That was when she'd met the Maddens. Her initial reaction to Orca Island had been love at first sight. Convincing her husband to visit had taken some work, but once Beau came with her for her sister Mia's wedding, he'd agreed Hearts Bay was the perfect place to settle down.

A tender ache throbbed behind her sternum. Oh, how she missed him. They'd bought the house and intended to use it as an investment property while Beau fulfilled his commitment to the army. She hated that he wouldn't be here to see their dream of living on an island become a reality.

Or ever know their child.

Blinking back tears, Lexi pushed through the exit and stepped out into the cool evening. The sun set much later here than back home. It would probably take her the rest of summer to adapt to the nearly twenty hours of daylight. It was after seven and golden rays still spilled across the lawn. People strolled along the sidewalks and families zipped by, riding bikes and scooters, soaking up the gorgeous weather.

Fumbling for her sunglasses, she found them in her bag and slipped them on. The Maddens had helped her buy a used vehicle. A sensible hatchback with plenty of room for a car seat and stroller. She'd parked a couple of blocks away and had walked to Town Hall for the meeting. Fatigue weighted her steps, but going home to her empty house without Beau was the last thing she wanted to do. Maybe taking a short walk would do her some good.

"Lexi?"

She turned toward the familiar voice. Tess, one of her sisters, walked toward her. Her husband, Asher, pushed a stroller with their daughter, Lucy, inside. Their son, Cameron, walked beside Tess, singing a song off-key.

"Hey." Lexi formed her mouth into a smile. "What are y'all up to?"

"We had pizza at The Tide Pool," Tess said. "Now Cam wants ice cream."

Cameron rolled his eyes and heaved a dramatic sigh. "Mom, please don't pretend I'm the only one who wants dessert. Will you come with us, Aunt Lexi?"

Lexi's heart expanded at his sweet invitation.

"I'd love to, but I've already had two cookies at my meeting."

"So?" Cameron's expression twisted in disbelief. "What's wrong with cookies and ice cream?"

Asher chuckled. "He's a tweenager. There's always plenty of space in his stomach for dessert."

"We're going to try the new ice cream truck." Tess pointed toward the white food truck parked nearby. Two turquoise tables were arranged on a patch of green grass. Seagulls soared overhead, cawing. A short line had formed from the truck's service window.

"That sounds fun," Lexi said.

"Want to join us?" Tess picked up the plastic rattle Lucy had chucked from the stroller and dropped it in the basket underneath. "We won't stay long because it's getting close to bedtime."

"Sure. Those cookies were small. Besides, I'm always in the mood for ice cream."

"Same." Tess looped her arm through Lexi's. They crossed the street and joined the end of the line.

Lucy jabbered from her seat inside the stroller. She wore a yellow T-shirt and denim shorts.

Lexi reached down and squeezed the toddler's bare leg. "Hey, sweet girl. How are you?"

"Dah!" Lucy grinned and pointed toward a beautiful husky dog sitting quietly at its owner's feet.

"Watch this, Lexi." Cameron let go of Asher's hand, then demonstrated a series of complicated kicks, punches and martial-arts moves that Lexi couldn't possibly name.

"Wow, supercool." She shot Asher a quick help-me-out-here glance. Boy, she had a lot to learn when it came to relating to children. Especially middle schoolers. How was she supposed to know what her son or daughter liked? What if he or she was into stuff she knew nothing about?

"You've got that deer-in-the-headlights expression," Asher said. "Don't worry. They aren't born asking to sign up for martial-arts classes."

"Yeah, kids just like to know we're paying attention." Tess inched the stroller forward as the line moved closer to the truck. "Cameron doesn't care if we know the names of all the moves. He wants us to watch and give him some encouragement."

The tension knotting the muscles between her shoulder blades loosened. "Now, that I can do. I'm good at encouraging people."

"You're going to be a great mom." Her sister gave Lexi's arm a gentle pat. "Believe me, I had to learn a whole lot in a short amount of time. God will give you the courage and stamina you'll need."

"I hope so."

Lexi hadn't lived in Hearts Bay or known the Maddens when Tess had found out she was Cameron's mother. It had been a few years, but Lexi had heard the story. Yet another thing Cameron wasn't shy about sharing. If anyone could relate to her worries about becoming a mom, it was Tess.

"What have you been up to lately?" Tess slid an elastic band from her wrist and secured her long dark hair in a loose ponytail. "I haven't seen you since last week."

"Actually, I've been dog sitting for my neighbor." Lexi fidgeted with the hot-pink tassel on her handbag. Talking about Heath and Scout to her sister made her feel uncertain.

"Really? You're offering pet-sitting services?"

"It's not what I'd planned on doing. His dog needs a lot of attention and keeps showing up in my yard, and I..." She trailed off, hesitating. Did she want to be this honest and vulnerable with her sister? "I need some money, so I couldn't say no."

Tess's eyes rounded. "Oh, dear. I didn't realize money was an issue."

Lexi looked away. "I have benefits from the military because Beau died in a training accident, but I want to save as much as I can. Photography clients are hard to come by around here since I'm so new."

"Is that what you're doing out here tonight? Taking pictures?"

She shook her head. "I went to the meeting about Fish Fest."

Before Tess could respond, Lucy squealed and started to fuss. Tess pulled back the stroller's visor, located the pacifier down in the stroller cushions and offered it to her. Lucy plucked it from her mom's hand, popped it in her mouth and leaned back.

"There." Tess straightened and glanced at Asher. "We're pushing our limits, keeping her out this late. We might have to take this ice cream to go."

"It'll be fine, babe." Asher dropped a quick kiss on the top of her head.

Lexi's heart pinched again. The Maddens had been so kind and accepting toward her, and for that she was eternally grateful. It had been awkward at first, when she'd claimed to be biologically linked to them through a wild switched-at-birth accident. But being welcomed into the family fold had helped soothe the sting when her parents in Georgia turned their backs on her after she'd decided to move here.

Their rejection on top of the loss of her husband had been a lot to process.

"Are you going to take part in the festival or did you sign up to volunteer?" Tess asked.

"My new neighbor—he's the guy who owns the dog— he's going to help me come up with a booth. I'm trying to get more photography clients before the baby's born."

"He sounds like a friendly neighbor. Anyone I know?" Her sister reached inside her diaper bag for her wallet.

"He's new to town. Heath Donovan. Works as a police officer."

"Hmm. Doesn't sound familiar." Tess motioned for Cameron to come closer. "Cam, it's almost time to order."

Lexi stepped up to the window and ordered a cup of vanilla ice cream with rainbow sprinkles. She paid, then carried her ice cream to one of the empty picnic tables.

Tess's questions had been harmless, but Lexi still felt uneasy. She wasn't doing anything wrong. Heath needed a dog sitter and she'd need his help building a booth for the festival. A fair trade. Beau had given his life for his country. He was one of the most loving, unselfish humans she'd ever known. If they'd been here together, they'd help a neighbor in need. And she'd honor his memory by providing their child with a secure future. It wasn't like she was the least bit interested in romance.

Chapter Three

Heath parked in his driveway and turned off the ignition. It had been a long week. He leaned back against the headrest and closed his eyes. Today he'd made his first arrest since he joined Hearts Bay's police department. On patrol this afternoon, he'd noticed a driver behaving erratically on Main Street. Heath had pulled the vehicle over for a traffic violation, then realized the driver was clearly intoxicated.

Arresting the belligerent man had created a scene, drawing an uncomfortable number of onlookers. Heath's partner, Jeff, had diffused the bystanders who'd gathered on the sidewalk outside the gift shop. The guy they'd arrested had resisted every step of the way. Taking him into the station and working through the standard operating procedure had taken much longer than Heath had anticipated.

He wiped his palm across his face. An ache throbbed in the center of his forehead. He hadn't been this exhausted after work in ages. Was this a sign that he was developing Huntington's symptoms? An icy chill tiptoed down his spine.

One tough day does not equal a fatal diagnosis.

His counselor back in Spokane had told him this multiple times. Sound wisdom and something Heath tried to remember anytime he worried about his health. He couldn't dwell on his struggles. A person who resisted arrest was part of his job. He wouldn't let it ruin his two days off. Grabbing his backpack, he climbed out of his truck and strode toward his front door.

As soon as he changed out of his uniform, he'd go over to Lexi's and pick up Scout. The guy scheduled to build his fence had delayed the project. Something about a supply-chain issue. That meant at least another week without a fenced yard.

He'd have to check in with Lexi and make sure she was still okay with taking care of Scout. Which he hoped was the case, because the pup's behavior had improved dramatically now that he was getting plenty of attention.

"What dog wouldn't be happy spending a whole day with Lexi?" He posed the question to his empty house as he stepped inside. Setting his backpack down by the hall closet, he squashed that notion as quickly as it flitted through his head. His thoughts turned to his pretty neighbor far too often.

He needed a distraction.

That was why he planned to stay busy this weekend. His house had been move-in ready, but he could always find something to tinker with. A spare bedroom to paint. At the staff meeting this week, his supervisor had reminded them that the festival was only three weeks away. So maybe he couldn't avoid Lexi completely—they had to discuss her plans for her festival booth, especially if he needed to build something for her—but he'd do his best to minimize their time together.

Heath changed quickly into jeans and a vintage T-shirt featuring his favorite baseball team. He shoved his feet into his tennis shoes, then walked next door and rang her doorbell. When she opened the door, he wasn't fully prepared for the way her wide smile made him feel like he'd just stepped into a ray of sunshine.

"Hey." She stepped back. "Come on in."

"Thanks." He barely squeezed the word past his dry throat. The tantalizing aroma of something delicious greeted him as he stepped inside. His stomach growled. A movie soundtrack streamed from a wireless speaker nearby.

"Scout's sound asleep." Lexi gestured toward the dog flopped on his side, curls concealing his eyes.

Heath surveyed the cozy space. "You have a velvet green sofa."

"Sure do." She tucked her hands in the pockets of her long blue dress. "Everyone told me the weather here was dreary, so I decided I'd fill my house with as much color as possible."

He turned in a slow circle. From the pillows on the sofa to the artwork on the walls and books on her shelves, she'd fully committed to a palette of green, coral and gold. "I'd say you nailed it."

"Thank you. I've had fun decorating."

His gaze landed on a framed photo of Lexi in her wedding dress standing beside a good-looking guy in uniform. He glanced away. "Scout behaved, I hope?"

"He was very well-behaved." She picked up a discarded toy—a stuffed shark—and tucked it into the plastic bucket Heath used to carry Scout's supplies back and forth. The dog sat up, his brown eyes tracking her movement. The tip of his tail wagged sheepishly.

Heath tucked his hands in his back pockets. "Would you tell me if he was giving you trouble?"

"Of course. We had a great day, didn't we, Scout?"

The tail tip wagging picked up speed.

"If I take him for plenty of short walks, he spends more time napping." Lexi added a plastic container of dog food to the bucket. "He ate some of his food, but not all of it. The rest is in here."

"Thanks." Heath gestured toward her dining room table. "What's all this? Did you find a client?"

A sophisticated camera, two lenses and a black carrying case sat in the center of the cream-colored oval table. She'd lined up a colorful map, two snack bars and a bottle of water beside the gear.

Lexi fidgeted with the long gold pendant she wore around her neck. "I met a woman at the information meeting for the festival. Mackenzie Jackson. She moved to Hearts Bay with her husband because he's stationed here with the Coast Guard. She wants to start a blog to keep her friends and family updated on what it's like to live in Alaska. Anyway, she asked me if I'd contribute photos of the island and I said yes. So tomorrow I'm going hiking. I'll take some pictures and hopefully she'll use them."

His scalp prickled. Oh, brother. He did not like the sound of that. "You're going hiking all by yourself?"

"That's the plan." Her smooth brow furrowed. "Why? Do you think that's a bad idea?"

"Yes, I do."

"How come?" she asked.

"It's summer in Alaska. There could be bears. You're pregnant. And carrying gear is heavy."

Amusement sparkled in her eyes. "You're more than welcome to come with me. Bring Scout. I'm leaving at noon."

So much for keeping to himself...

"If you're busy, don't worry about it." She turned toward the table and carefully placed the lenses inside the bag. "I bought some bear spray and I'll tie some bells on my shoes or something. That's what the guy who sold me the bear spray said I should do."

Heath swallowed back an impatient sigh. "Those are things you're supposed to do, but I'd really prefer that you not go alone."

"Like I said, you and Scout are more than welcome to join me. Bears are probably terrified of Goldendoodles." She laughed, then zipped up the camera bag.

Why didn't she take this more seriously? "I have nothing going on tomorrow."

"Great." A timer on her phone rang. "Oh, the chicken enchiladas are ready. Would you like to stay for dinner? There's plenty."

Yes.

"It's been a long day. I'd better head home. Thanks again for dog sitting. Let's go, Scout."

The stubborn dog didn't budge.

"Scout." Heath snapped his fingers and pinned him with a pointed look. "Let's go."

The dog whined, then pushed to his feet. Head hanging low, he ambled toward the door.

Lexi bit her lip, obviously trying not to laugh. She handed Heath the bucket and Scout's leash. "See you tomorrow."

"See you." Heath attached the leash to Scout's collar and grabbed the bucket. Lexi opened the door and Heath stepped outside. "C'mon, buddy."

Lexi closed the door behind them. Tugging gently on the leash, he led Scout across the yard. "Time to give Lexi some space."

But how in the world was he going to hike with his neighbor and remain completely disinterested? Heath blew out a breath. Hopefully, focusing on their differences would be enough to keep him from entertaining foolish notions about the two of them. After all, they *were* polar opposites. She had an optimistic outlook, a stunning smile and the frilliest, most feminine house he'd ever seen. And he couldn't be certain, but that had sounded like a musical streaming on her speaker.

Scout plodded along. A bunny darted behind some bushes and Scout didn't even raise his snout. Sighing, Heath reached down and scratched behind Scout's ears. "I know, buddy… I'd like to stay longer, too."

But he couldn't. No matter how much he enjoyed Lexi's company, he couldn't risk a romantic relationship with someone who'd only get hurt.

"Perfect hiking weather, right?" Lexi said the next day, gently lowering her camera bag onto the driveway. "Not too hot. Not too cold. No rain in the forecast."

Heath didn't answer as he opened the passenger door on his truck. Scout shoved his head through the opening and barked.

She stole a glance at Heath. He had barely said a word other than hello when she'd stepped outside a few minutes ago. No worries. His sullen mood wouldn't dampen her excitement. Stretching her arms wide, she tipped her head back and drew in a deep breath. Sunshine peeked through the mottled clouds and warmed her skin. Birds chirped in the trees. Fresh air filled her lungs.

"Thank You, Lord, for a beautiful day." She'd been in such a hurry to get to church this morning that gratitude hadn't exactly been top of mind. But every new day was a gift. She'd try to be better at remembering that.

"I'd offer to take your bag, but you'd better keep it up front with you and away from Scout."

Heath's deep, smooth voice prodded her from her thoughts. Dropping her arms to her sides, she scooped up the bag and headed for the truck. "Good idea."

As she slid into the passenger seat and Heath closed the door, she caught a faint scent of something masculine. Like pine trees mixed with soap.

Scout's tongue swiped at her cheek, and she laughed.

"Hey, big fella." She set her gear between her feet, then twisted around and gave Scout a generous pat. "Ready for a fun adventure?"

Panting, Scout pinged back and forth in the narrow extended cab. Heath circled around to the driver's side, then slid behind the wheel.

Lexi buckled her seat belt. "Your car is so clean. What's your secret?"

There wasn't a speck of dirt or dust anywhere on the gray upholstery or center console. He had a tube of ChapStick stashed in the small alcove near the stick shift. No napkins, gum wrappers or receipts. Impressive.

Note to self. Clean out car before letting Heath see the inside.

"I like to keep things neat." He slid his dark sunglasses into place. "Messes make me nervous."

Oh, boy. Good thing he hadn't come inside her house just now. Last night's impromptu baking session had not gone as planned. She'd attempted to make energy bites for their hike. They'd tasted like cardboard. The ingredients for the abandoned project were still on the counter, plus dirty dishes filled her sink. She quickly surveyed his outfit. "And you're dressed for an expedition. Did I wear the right thing?"

Heath dipped his chin. He wore khaki cargo-style nylon pants with zippers and a dozen pockets. Probably the kind that transformed into shorts. Or carried his stash of climbing gear to summit the nearest mountain. She glimpsed a gray T-shirt under his plaid button-down, and he wore a vest layered over that. Was he expecting a surprise summer snowstorm? Did that even happen here?

He started the truck. "The weather can shift abruptly. I wanted to be prepared."

She glanced down at her own outfit. Should she run inside and change? She'd found a white T-shirt in her drawer that wasn't too snug. Her sneakers would have to do because she didn't own hiking boots. Black leggings were the most comfortable thing to wear these days. At the last minute she'd grabbed a long-sleeved chambray shirt and tied it around her waist. "Do you think I'm not prepared?"

A muscle in his jaw flexed. He hesitated, his hand on the gearshift. "Did you bring anything besides your camera gear? A rain poncho? Sunscreen? Snacks?"

"I put sunscreen on my face and I have sunglasses right here." She touched her favorite pair nestled on top of her head. "Oh, and I'm pretty sure I packed the granola bars."

"I have extra bottles of water and a few energy bars."

She rubbed her palms together. "Then we're all set. Let's do this."

His expression remained unreadable behind those dark sunglasses. Scout's panting filled the silence as Heath backed out of the driveway.

"Do you want to stop for coffee?" she asked.

"Is that what you want to do?"

"The coffee at The Trading Post is out-of-this-world delicious." She grinned at him. "Have you tried it yet?"

Heath shook his head.

"Oh, man. The white chocolate mochas are my favorite. It's on Main Street. I'll show you when we get closer."

"I know where it is." Heath turned on his blinker, then slowed to a stop at the end of their street. He looked both directions twice before turning right.

He was certainly a cautious driver. Maybe every police officer obeyed the laws. Not that she blew through stop signs or anything, but she certainly didn't pause for the required three seconds.

Scout whined, then finally sat down. Lexi fidgeted with the buttons on the cuff of her shirt. Heath stared straight ahead, keeping the car at exactly twenty-five miles per hour, hands at nine and three on the steering wheel. She'd spent a ridiculous amount of time online researching which trail she wanted to try first. Maybe Heath had a better hike in mind, though. He certainly had opinions about their outing.

She cleared her throat. "I've heard this trail leads to

one of the best viewpoints on the whole island. It's only two miles. Have you hiked around Mount Larsen?"

"I haven't done much hiking yet."

"Are you okay if we start with that trail?" she asked. "I read several comments in some online posts. I think I'll get the best pictures from the scenic viewpoint."

"This new friend of yours, who you met at the information meeting, is she paying you for your time?"

Lexi looked away. "We didn't discuss the terms. It's not really a formal agreement."

"You're going to let her use your pictures and not charge anything?"

"I'm hoping she'll love the pictures so much that she'll tell her friends," she admitted. "Then they'll tell their friends, and before I know it, I'll have a bunch of new clients who want to have their family's picture taken for their holiday cards. Word of mouth is a powerful marketing tool, you know."

"True."

She shot him another glance. *True?* As in he approved or he thought her plan was stupid? Stifling a sigh, she squirmed in her seat. His opinions shouldn't matter this much.

A few minutes later, he turned onto Main Street and stopped in front of The Trading Post. "I'll wait here," he said.

Scout yipped and pressed his paws onto the center console.

"Scout, no." Heath gently nudged the dog out of the way.

"Oh, come inside." Lexi unbuckled her seat belt. "The shop is adorable, and Annie, the owner, is supersweet. Besides, Scout loves the blizzards."

Heath's mouth twisted into a frown. "You've been giving my dog ice cream?"

"No, silly. It's a tiny cup full of whipped cream. Scout loves it."

"So you've been feeding my dog dairy products without my permission?"

Her stomach sank. "It was only one time. I should have asked your permission. I didn't realize your dog was dairy-free. I'm so sorry."

Rats. She was a terrible pet sitter. Goldendoodles had sensitive tummies. She knew this. Why hadn't she been more careful? "Scout didn't get sick, did he?"

"Not since he's been staying with you." Heath turned off the ignition. "You're sure dogs are allowed inside?"

"Scout is. Annie's his biggest fan."

His lips quirked. "I had no idea my pet had become a local celebrity."

The car rocked and bounced as Scout strained toward the door, his high-pitched yips making Lexi smile.

"All right, all right." Heath climbed out, then secured Scout's leash before flipping the seat forward. Scout bounded out of the vehicle and onto the sidewalk. He gave his whole body a thorough shake, then pranced toward Lexi.

She led the way toward the coffee shop's entrance. When she opened the door and stepped inside, Annie smiled and waved behind the counter. The bean grinder whirred, filling the air with the pungent aroma of fresh coffee.

"I brought your favorite Goldendoodle," Lexi called out.

Annie turned off the grinder, then rounded the corner of the counter. "Hi, Scout."

Scout sat down beside Heath, his head upturned, ready to receive Annie's greeting.

She dried her hands on the towel tucked into her apron, then patted his head.

"Annie, this is my friend Heath. Scout belongs to him. Heath, this is Annie. She owns The Trading Post."

Heath anchored his sunglasses on his vest pocket, then shook Annie's outstretched hand. "Nice to meet you, Annie."

"You, as well, Heath. You've got a great dog there."

Heath's smile didn't quite reach his eyes. "He has his moments."

"What can I get started for you?"

Lexi stepped toward the counter, her wallet in hand. "May I please have a decaf tall nonfat white chocolate mocha with an extra pump of chocolate and no whip?"

"Coming right up. I'll give your whipped cream to Scout." Annie reached for a cup from the stack beside the espresso machine and wrote Lexi's order on the side with a black marker. "And for you, Heath?"

"A small black coffee, please," he said.

"Wow, you really walk on the wild side," Lexi teased, eyeing the fresh cookies and muffins displayed inside the glass bakery case.

"That's how I like my coffee." Heath roped Scout's leash around his forearm, keeping the dog firmly positioned at his side. "I'm not comfortable bringing my unruly animal inside a coffee shop."

Lexi straightened. Man, was he going to rain on her parade the entire day? "You can wait outside if you'd like. I'll bring our drinks out when they're ready."

Heath studied her. "I'm not going to let you buy my coffee."

Oh, brother. Grumpy *and* old-fashioned. She ignored his comment and waved to the customers she recognized sitting at the closest table, an older couple who owned the local hardware store. "Good morning. It's nice to see you again. I put that snake plant in my kitchen like you suggested, and it seems quite content."

The woman dabbed at her mouth with her napkin, then reached for her coffee. "So glad to hear that, dear. Come by anytime. We're here to help."

Heath fumbled for his wallet. "Do you know everyone in town?"

"Not yet," Lexi said cheerfully. "Give me another couple of weeks."

Scout yipped, earning an exasperated glance from Heath.

"Want me to hold the leash while you pay?"

"Please." Heath handed her the leash, then fished out his debit card. "Would you like anything to eat?"

"Since you offered, those blueberry muffins look yummy."

"Done."

After Heath paid, Annie handed them a white paper bag, a cardboard carton with their drinks and a tiny cup of whipped cream for Scout.

Outside, Scout nearly barreled into a young couple coming into the shop. "Easy, fella." Lexi steered him to a black wrought iron table and two chairs. Scout sat down on the narrow patch of grass beside the table, whining.

"I won't give Scout this whipped cream if you don't want him to have it," Lexi said.

Heath shrugged. "It's fine. Go ahead."

"Here you go, buddy." Lexi plucked the tiny cup

from the holder and held it out. He scooped out the whipped cream with his tongue, devouring the treat in a few seconds.

Heath released a low whistle. "Nicely done."

Lexi sat down but Heath remained standing, still holding the muffins and coffee. "Take a load off," she told him.

His lips flattened. He set the drinks and the bag on the table. Then he sat down in the chair opposite hers. Scout sank to all fours, heaved a loud sigh, then rested his snout on his paws.

The bag crinkled in her hands. She took the muffins out and set them on the napkins Annie had tucked inside. Plump blueberries, sugar sprinkled on top and the sweet aroma made her mouth water. "These look amazing. Here."

He slid the napkin with the muffin closer. She retrieved her coffee from the tray, eyeing him. "You're not a stop-and-smell-the-roses kind of guy, are you?"

His cheeks reddened. "No."

"We're going hiking. In one of the most beautiful places on earth. This is supposed to be fun, but you look like a kid who just lost their screen-time privileges. What's up with that?"

Heath hesitated, his coffee cup halfway to his mouth. "I'm more of a glass-half-empty kind of guy."

Shocker.

She stopped short of taking another jab at him. Something prodded her to go easy on the guy. Maybe he'd endured the unimaginable, too.

He might've lived through a hard season, but still, she refused to let his solemn demeanor drag her down. He'd insisted on coming along, convinced she couldn't stay safe without him keeping watch. She'd make him laugh today if it was the last thing she did.

How could one short hike make him so nervous?

Heath stopped walking and swiped his arm across the moisture on his forehead. Scout tugged on the leash, determined to tunnel even deeper into the raspberry bushes beside the trail.

"No, Scout." He redirected the dog back onto the dirt path leading toward a canopy of spruce trees.

"This view is stunning." Lexi had stopped a few steps ahead, her camera poised to snap another picture. "Everything is so green and lush. I can't get over it."

The last of the morning fog had evaporated. Sun warmed his skin. Through breaks in the trees, he glimpsed the blue-green water stretching toward the horizon. Lexi was right. The views from the trail were incredible. He'd try not to stress when she stopped every fifteen feet to take another picture.

She lowered the camera and stared at the screen on the back, cycling through the photos she'd taken. He loosened the cap on his water bottle and took a long pull. Had she drunk any water? He noted the flush on her cheeks. The hike was steeper than he'd expected. She'd sounded winded a time or two, but he'd kept his observations to himself. At the coffee shop, he'd sensed he'd irritated her.

"Do you need to drink some water?" He twisted the cap back on his container and stowed it in his pack. "Or eat another snack?"

Her expression turned sheepish. "I'll get some water after I take this picture."

Fair enough. He shifted his attention back to Scout,

who'd discovered a tree branch. He sat beside Heath's feet, gnawing on one end.

Lexi's breath hitched. "Look."

Heath turned. She dropped her voice to a whisper. "Bald eagle."

Her camera clicked and whirred. The regal bird sat perched in the top of a spruce tree. Its white head, hooked yellow beak and dark brown feathers contrasted against the evergreen forest backdrop.

Scout released a low growl, then slowly stood. Heath glanced down. "What is it, pal?"

The fur on the back of Scout's neck rose, and his ears perked up.

Fear danced along Heath's spine. Something crashed through the brush up ahead. Adrenaline surged through his veins. He stretched out his hand toward Lexi, determined to shield her from whatever danger lurked.

"Behind me. Now." The words came out more harshly than he'd intended.

She lowered her camera and turned slowly, eyes wide. "What's wrong?"

Scout growled again, then crouched low.

"There's something in the trees," he whispered. "Get behind me."

She scampered closer and stood behind him.

Tree branches rustled and cracked. Movement through the trees made Heath's mouth run dry. Scout's bark shifted to a bellow.

They'd tied bells to their packs and he had bear spray, but he'd left his handgun in the safe at home. A choice he regretted now. If a grizzly bear with cubs came out of the woods, they were in a heap of trouble.

A deer and two fawns emerged from the forest. They

picked their way carefully around the foliage, then ambled onto the trail. Lexi snickered.

Irritation knifed at him. He'd made her safety his priority. She obviously wasn't taking this seriously.

Scout barked, his tail wagging. The deer sprang into action, their long spindly legs carrying them off into the woods again.

Heath's shoulders sagged. He knelt beside Scout and tunneled his fingers through the dog's curly hair. "Good boy. Way to stay alert."

Scout angled his head toward Heath's and licked his face.

He turned to check on Lexi. She stood with one hand clamped over her mouth. Her body shook with laughter.

Heath narrowed his gaze. "Laugh all you want. If that had been a mama bear and her cubs, you'd be running for your life."

"I'm sorry." She drew a calming breath. "Really, I am. I shouldn't have laughed."

His heart still kicked against his ribs. He tightened his grip on Scout's leash.

Lexi's expression grew serious. Worry filled her golden-brown eyes. "You look pale. Are you okay?"

He averted his gaze, pretending to check on the deer's location. He didn't want to admit the truth. Especially when he'd made such a big deal of keeping her safe. "I'm terrified of bears."

"Oh, my." She moved closer. "Did you have a bad experience?"

If only. At least that would justify his phobia. He hung his head. "Nope. I saw a show on television when I was younger, and I've been scared ever since."

"You know you've moved to an island that's world-famous for having the largest bears, right?"

"I'm aware," Heath muttered, scraping his hiking boot over a rock protruding from the ground. He felt like a child, confessing his fear. She must think he was an idiot.

"We can go." She lifted the strap on her camera from around her neck.

"You didn't get all the pictures that you wanted."

"It's fine. I can come again some other time." She held up her palm. "Not by myself. I know that freaks you out."

"But you wanted a picture of the waterfall. That's all you talked about when we were driving here from the coffee shop."

"Yeah, it would be a shame to turn back without seeing that…" She pulled her map from the side pocket of her bag. "We're super close. I promise, once we see the waterfall, we'll turn around and go straight back to the truck. No more pictures."

Laughter rumbled from his chest. "You don't mean that."

"Hey, you laughed." She pumped the air with her fist. "That was one of my personal objectives today."

"For real?"

"Yep." She jammed the map back inside the pocket. "You have a nice laugh, by the way."

He straightened, her compliment swirling around him. She liked his laugh?

"C'mon. This way." Lexi strode up the trail. Scout followed, his tail bobbing like a flag in the breeze. Heath fell in behind them, keeping his hand fisted around the leash handle.

Lexi chatted away. She stopped frequently to take pictures with her phone and her fancy camera. He tried to be patient. She just kept talking, telling him about her adventures camping in the Georgia mountains as a child. He only half listened, his radar on high alert. Ready to defend her. What was it about Lexi that made him feel so fiercely protective? He'd never felt this concerned about a woman in his life.

The sound of water trickling over rocks grew louder.

"We're almost there," she called over her shoulder. "It's right around this curve."

They followed the dirt path through the forest until it wound around a rocky outcropping.

"Oh, it's beautiful." Lexi slowed her steps. "I'm going to move closer to the creek for a better angle."

"Wait." Heath scanned the path leading down toward the edge of the creek. Rocks and mud formed an uneven, sloped surface. "Can't you take the picture from here?"

"I'll be careful, I promise." She flashed him a smile over her shoulder, squeezing the air from his lungs. What he wouldn't give to have even an ounce of her cupcakes-and-confetti zest for life.

He trained his gaze on her feet. Trampled grass hinted that plenty of other people had made the trek down to the creek. She set her bag on the ground, then inched closer, grasping her camera in one hand, the strap looped around her neck.

"Please don't fall," he gritted out. Scout barked, straining against the leash, then turned back and gave Heath an are-you-going-to-let-this-happen look.

"I know. I'm watching."

Scout whined and sat down, leaning against Heath's

leg. The air was thick with moisture. Tree branches overhead formed a dense canopy, shielding them from the sun. The waterfall spilled over rocks, splashing into the creek below and kicking spray into the air. Seeing the waterfall and knowing Lexi could get the pictures she wanted softened the edges of his anxiety. They'd be back at the truck shortly and he could stop worrying.

Scout lunged, yanking Heath off balance. He spun around, wincing as Scout's momentum wrenched his shoulder. "Scout, no!"

His backpack slipped, and Heath struggled to keep his grip on the leash. Scout barked at a squirrel scampering up a tree.

Lexi's yelp pierced the air. He turned in time to see her slip off the muddy rocks and stumble into the creek.

Chapter Four

"I still have my camera." Lexi thrust her prized possession high in the air. Thankfully, she'd secured the strap around her neck. She'd slipped and fallen so quickly that there hadn't been time to do much more than put her hand out to brace her fall.

She sloshed toward the side of the creek bed, wincing at the sharp pain in her foot. Her wet leggings clung to her skin, and water dripped from the shirt she'd tied around her waist.

"Give me your hand." Heath stood on the muddy shore, his legs spread wide, Scout's leash twined around his ropy, muscular forearm. The grim line of his mouth and the granitelike clenched jaw hinted at his disapproval.

"I'm fine." She refused to take his hand, and then she stumbled again. Icy water had filled her sneakers and made them feel a thousand times heavier. The sharp pain around the outside of her foot wasn't easing up at all.

"Lexi, give me your hand. You're soaked."

"Not completely."

Goodness, she sounded like a petulant child. Reluctantly, she took his hand, allowing him to guide her carefully across the slippery mud and uneven rocks that had instigated her fall.

Even though her stubborn, prideful side hated to accept help.

Heath's warm grip and the ease with which he pulled her to safety weakened her resolve not to need him.

"You fell hard on that arm. Are you sure you're okay?"

She eased her fingers from his as soon as she was on dry ground, then gingerly rotated her wrist. Her elbow throbbed and she had a scrape on her palm. She must've fallen on a sharp rock in the water.

Not that she would admit that to him.

"I'm fine." No need to mention the pain in her foot, either. She swiped her hand on her damp leggings, then carefully examined her camera. Using the only dry portion of her T-shirt's hem, she wiped droplets of water from the screen on the back.

Scout yipped and lunged toward her again, planting his muddy paws on her leg. His soulful brown eyes met hers. What a sweet animal.

"No, Scout. Sit." Heath pulled the dog back.

Scout whimpered and sank to his haunches, tongue lolling.

Lexi pressed the power button on her camera. She'd take one quick picture to make sure it worked, and then they'd hike back to the truck. Except nothing happened. Oh, no. Her stomach pitted with dread. All her plans for the festival, the photos she'd taken for her new friend and her grand idea to use today's trek to generate new customers—it would all be for nothing if she'd ruined her camera.

Emotion burned the back of her throat. Beau had bought her new photography equipment after they were engaged. A generous gift and a gesture she'd treasured. One that meant even more now that he was gone.

She gulped back a sob. "I—I think my camera might have taken on too much water."

A muscle in Heath's cheek twitched. "What's important is that you're not injured. Are you sure you're all right?"

"I said I'm fine." She pushed out the words and didn't bother to hide her exasperation. He couldn't bring himself to say one word about her camera. No "Sorry to hear that" or "Wow, that's too bad"?

Anger welled, but she refused to let any tears fall. Not now. Not in front of Heath. He probably thought she was such a fool, tripping over her own two feet and falling in less than a foot of slow-moving water. She had gotten some good shots of the waterfall. Even if her camera was ruined, hopefully the storage card inside could be recovered. She'd hate to have to admit to her friend that today had been a bust.

"Let's head back to the truck." Heath turned and started for the trail.

She clenched her jaw to keep her teeth from chattering. There was no point in arguing with him. Scout fell into step beside him, then stopped, looked back at Lexi and barked.

"I'm right behind you."

Well, sort of. That stupid pain in her foot slowed her down. She willed her body to cooperate. Maybe she'd twisted something in her effort to preserve her camera.

Her palm instinctively went to her abdomen. Hopefully her little one hadn't been impacted by the fall. The thought sent an icy jolt of terror straight through her. It all had happened so fast. One minute she'd captured the perfect photo of the silvery white water spilling over the rocks carved out of the lush green hillside. The next second her feet had slipped and she'd landed on her backside in the stream. Now her sneakers made a squishy sound with every step.

Heath stopped and turned back. "What's wrong?"

"Nothing. Just taking my time."

She tried to walk without limping under his piercing gaze.

"You're hurt."

"My foot's a little sore. We can keep going."

Heath stopped walking and slipped off his backpack. "Here. Hold the leash. Please."

Lexi took Scout's leash, then leaned over and gave the dog a generous head scratch. Scout tipped his snout up and licked her cheek. "What are you doing?"

"I'm getting you an extra sweatshirt and my emergency splint kit."

She eyed the backpack. He carried emergency splints in that thing? Another tremor racked her body. "Let's keep walking. We're not that far from—"

Heath gave her an oh-please-you're-not-fooling-me look.

"I guess I am a little cold. Thank you." She took the sweatshirt, handed him Scout's leash and pulled the thick cotton fabric over her head. It dropped almost to the middle of her thighs. Wow, it smelled good, too. Like soap and the outdoors.

Stop. She mentally drop-kicked that thought into the

creek. This was not the time to think about how good he smelled. She was a pregnant widow. Beau hadn't been gone all that long. A new relationship was out of the question.

"Look." She rotated her ankle in a slow circle. "I can move it. Nothing's broken. Let's keep going."

Heath's lips flattened into a grim line. He hesitated, then dropped the bright orange contraption back inside his bag. "If you say so. Will you at least let me carry your camera?"

"That's probably a good idea." She lifted the strap from around her neck, then handed the camera over. He tucked it inside her bag. Then he put his backpack on, hooked her camera bag over his shoulder and tugged Scout toward him.

Gritting her teeth against the sharp pain along the outside of her foot, she limped along the trail. Man, she was an idiot. This was a huge mistake. What had she been thinking—moving here, trying to be a helpful neighbor and pretending she could start over on an island in the middle of the ocean? Shame washed over her. What if her foolish notions harmed her little one?

He had to convince Lexi to see a doctor. Today.

"I can tell by the way you're limping that you're injured. Why don't you let me take you to the emergency room?"

"Absolutely not." She huffed out a breath as she leaned against his truck. "I'm fine."

He studied her. Perspiration dotted her brow and tight lines around her mouth indicated she was anything but fine.

"Please, just take me home."

He swallowed a groan. So stubborn. "All right."

Keeping a firm grasp on Scout's leash, Heath moved past her and opened the passenger door on his truck. Scout sat on the ground and leaned against Heath's leg, panting. As if he sensed there was a problem.

"Good boy." He reached down and gave the Golden-doodle a scratch on the head. If only Scout could some-how convince Lexi she needed to get checked out.

"Here, let me get you a towel." He reached behind her seat and pulled out a rolled-up towel he kept stashed there for emergencies, then handed it to her. "I have a thermal blanket if you need it."

She took the towel and shook her head. "No blan-ket. The towel works. Thanks."

He waited, prepared to intervene if she couldn't get in the truck. Slowly, she maneuvered onto the passen-ger seat. Her expression crimped and she sucked air through her teeth.

His chest tightened. Scout whined. What if she had a more significant injury than a possible broken bone? Her fall hadn't been that traumatic. Still, he'd feel bet-ter if she had an exam by a medical professional. She turned and reached for the seat belt.

"Is there any particular reason why you don't want to see a doctor?" He stood beside the open door, one hand gripping the frame, the other keeping Scout's leash wound taut around his wrist.

"Because I don't need to." She glared at him. "I slipped and fell in the creek. I'm soaking wet and a little sore, but I'll be good as new in a few days." She clicked the buckle into place, then held out her hand. "I'll take my camera, please."

A few *days*? His mind instantly jumped to worst-case scenarios, with visions of her all alone on her green sofa, unable to get help or manage her pain. He wouldn't be able to sleep at night, knowing she might be next door feeling miserable.

But he couldn't make her do something she didn't want to do.

He handed her the camera bag, then closed the passenger door and guided the dog around the vehicle to the driver's side. Scout pranced beside him, still whining.

"I know, buddy. How can we help her?" Heath reached down and gave Scout another encouraging pat, then opened his door and pulled the seat forward. Scout leaped inside.

Heath unclipped the leash and stashed his backpack. The canine pushed through the gap in the seats, planted both paws on the console and licked Lexi's cheek.

She chuckled and twisted in her seat, giving Scout a thorough ear scratch. "You're a good boy, you know that? I'm sorry I ruined our fun."

Heath shot her a look as he slipped behind the wheel. "You didn't ruin anything."

Lexi stared straight ahead, clutching her camera bag. "I hate that my clumsiness cut our hike short."

"Accidents happen. Don't be too hard on yourself." He turned on the ignition but didn't shift the truck into gear. "You've mentioned having family on the island. Is there anyone who can come and stay with you?"

Irritation flashed in her eyes. "You're not going to let this go, are you?"

Wow, this was exasperating. He squeezed the steering wheel with both hands. "What if your foot's broken? You can't keep hobbling around on it, hoping that it will randomly heal itself."

"I'm not hoping it will randomly heal itself." She squirmed in her seat. "Look, I feel stupid enough already. I don't need you making me feel worse."

Ouch. Her words stung. "Is that what you think I'm doing? Trying to make you feel guilty? I'm a police officer, Lexi. I'm trained to assist people when they're dealing with a crisis."

"This isn't a crisis."

He held up his palm in a desperate attempt to keep from arguing. Again. "It goes against my nature and my professional responsibilities to drop you off in your house knowing that you might need medical attention."

"All right. You win." She plucked her phone from her bag. "I'll text one of my sisters and let them know what's going on. If they're not busy, maybe they'll come and hang with me."

Hang out with her? Not quite the answer he was looking for. He was hoping she'd say that she'd let one of them take her to the emergency room. Swallowing his displeasure, he clicked his seat belt into place, then glanced at her again. He wasn't going to let his exasperation show. Nope. The right thing to do was to be extra patient and attentive.

Her annoyed gaze pinged between him and her phone. "Why aren't you going anywhere?"

"I'm waiting for you to tell me that you have someone to stay with you. I can't leave you home alone knowing that you might have an injury."

She quirked her lips to one side. "Then I'll text Mia. She's a physician assistant. She'll know what to do."

He sagged against his seat and loosened his grip on the steering wheel. "Great idea."

Scout let out a yip, then stuck his nose between the seats and licked Lexi's cheek again.

Attaboy.

Lexi rewarded him with a soft smile and another gentle pat. "Don't worry, Scout. Everything's going to be fine."

Scout whined, then smacked his lips. His big head swiveled toward Heath with an are-you-seeing-this-right-now look in his big brown eyes.

"We're getting this sorted, big guy." Heath tunneled his fingers into the dense curls around Scout's neck.

Thankfully, his dog remembered his manners and sat down, but he kept a watchful eye on Lexi.

Outside, soupy fog had rolled in and rain pattered against the windshield.

Lexi's phone pinged. "I sent a group text. Mia didn't answer but Rylee did. She's pretty sure Mia's working in the ER at the hospital and suggested I go straight there."

Heath resisted pumping the air with his fist. No need to gloat. "Perfect. Let's go."

Lexi said nothing more as they drove toward Hearts Bay Community Hospital. His windshield wipers thwacked out a steady rhythm. He mentally scrolled through a list of inane topics. Small talk wasn't his gift, though. She was clearly irritated with him for looking out for her best interests. Which aggravated him, because he genuinely wanted to help. Besides, her camera might be broken. And it was his dog that had lunged for that dumb squirrel. No, it wasn't his fault that she fell, but he still felt somewhat responsible. He admired her strength and her fierce determination to remain independent.

But if she had a broken foot, she was going to need a whole lot more help. Someone helping her design a booth for a festival would be the least of her worries.

"Broken? Seriously?"

Lexi stared in disbelief at the film Mia had clipped onto the light box mounted on the wall. Out in the hallway, shoes squeaked on the linoleum floor and muffled voices filtered through the drawn curtain separating her cubby from the rest of the hospital's emergency area. Blood roared in Lexi's head. What was she going to do now?

Mia Colman tapped her manicured fingertip against the X-ray of Lexi's right foot. "That fifth metatarsal has a hairline fracture."

"My fifth meta-what?" Lexi fought to keep her voice from trembling. Not that she couldn't cry in front of Mia. After discovering they'd been switched at birth when they were newborns, they'd become quite close. But if she started bawling now, Lexi wasn't sure she'd stop anytime soon.

Mia plucked the X-ray from the box and tucked it inside a large envelope. "It's the long bone that connects your little toe to your ankle. Hairline means it's a tiny crack, as opposed to the kind of fracture where a piece of bone breaks off."

She shivered involuntarily. "That doesn't sound good."

"It's a common place for a bone to break, especially when someone slips and falls." Mia offered an empathetic smile. "When is your next prenatal visit?"

Her breath seized in her lungs. "I thought you said my foot's broken. Are you worried about my baby?"

"No." Mia gently rested her hand on Lexi's arm. "I'm not worried about the fall. But, typically, a pregnant woman sees her provider between sixteen and eighteen weeks, so you're due for an appointment soon. It's my job to make sure my ER patients are getting the care they need."

"I—I'm sorry." Lexi wrinkled her nose. "This whole day's been super stressful. I didn't mean to overreact. Thank you for asking me. I'm supposed to see Dr. Rasmussen next week."

"Excellent." Mia stepped back and pulled the wheeled cart holding a computer toward her. "He's a phenomenal physician. I know he'll take great care of you."

"I hope so." She winced. Wow, her foot was really starting to hurt. The white paper on the exam table wrinkled as she scooted back and extended her legs in front of her. "So, what are my options for fixing a fracture?"

Mia studied the computer screen. "I know this is a hassle. The good news is, we have lots of people on the island that care about you and are willing to help."

Images of Heath helping her navigate the muddy creek bed and pulling an emergency splint kit from his backpack filled her head. Again, she pushed aside anything that made her think of him.

"The first step is immobilization," Mia continued. "That will control pain and help stabilize the bone and give it a chance to heal."

"Does that mean a cast?" Lexi lay down on the table and flung her arm across her forehead. Yeah, okay, that was a little dramatic, but she did not want to spend the rest of the summer gimping around on crutches with a bulky plaster thing.

"Not a cast. We'll fit you for a walking boot."

"Please tell me you're joking. Those things are hideous."

"Believe it or not, the walking boot is the better choice. You don't have to worry about it getting wet. Of course, driving will be tricky with a boot on, so I recommend you not—"

"No *driving*?" Lexi pushed up on both elbows. "I'll have to ask for help with almost everything."

Mia paused, her fingers hovering over her keyboard. "Sounds like you have a thoughtful neighbor. Maybe he can help?"

Lexi sighed, then sat up slowly. That was the problem. She didn't want to ask Heath for help. But she wasn't getting into that with Mia right now. Yes, she and Mia, along with Tess, Rylee and their parents, had formed a strong bond over the last year. But still, she wasn't quite ready to open up about the complicated matter of navigating life as a widowed mom-to-be with them.

Or admit to her growing attachment to her handsome neighbor.

Sure, Heath had demonstrated that he was trustworthy and conscientious. And she was fortunate to have him living next door. But that didn't mean she wanted him waiting on her constantly for the rest of the summer. Their dog-sitting and festival-prep arrangement was quite enough, thank you very much.

"Lexi?"

"Hmm?"

Mia's mouth curved into a knowing smile. "I think

you tuned out for a second. I said we'll repeat the X-ray in a few weeks and see how the bone is healing. If it's not, I'll have to refer you to an orthopedic surgeon off the island."

Off island? She'd have to buy a plane ticket. Or else endure a long ferry ride. "That sounds expensive."

"If the bone doesn't heal while you're wearing the boot, then we'll have to try another method to encourage healing."

"Does that mean surgery?" Lexi's voice wobbled. She fiddled with the hem of Heath's bulky sweatshirt. "Can a pregnant woman have anesthesia?"

Add that to her list of things she didn't have a clue about.

"I was thinking more in terms of a bone growth stimulator, but sometimes it can be difficult to get insurance to approve that. Let's try the boot. I recommend wearing it when you're awake and taking it easy. My assistant will be in shortly with the boot and your paperwork for checkout." Mia stood. "Any questions?"

Lexi shook her head, then fisted her hands in her lap. This day was getting worse by the hour.

"I'm sorry I didn't have better news. It's great to see you." Mia leaned in and gave Lexi a quick hug. "Text me anytime if you think of questions or if your pain gets worse."

Lexi forced a smile. "Thank you."

Mia pushed her cart out of the exam area, then tugged the curtain closed. Lexi stared at a diagram of the human body mounted on the wall. She'd never broken a bone before. Or had any major health issues. She'd really wanted to enjoy the rest of the summer, exploring the island, building her business and preparing for her baby's arrival in December.

Now she was forced to slow down so her foot healed properly.

Her phone hummed with an incoming text, temporarily jarring her out of her misery. She plucked it from the table.

I took Scout home. Now I'm sitting in the waiting room. Any news?

She pressed her fingers to her lips. Oh, he was being so kind.

Fractured bone near the outside of my foot. 5th metasomething. I have to wear a boot for six weeks. No surgery unless the bone doesn't heal.

She added a barfing face emoji, then sent the message to Heath.

The dots on her screen bounced. Then stopped. Bounced again. She couldn't look away. Why did she care so much about a text message? He was literally right down the hall in the waiting room.

Heath's new text popped up on her phone.

It could be worse. You're a strong woman. Wearing a boot for a few weeks isn't so bad.

Lexi set her phone down without answering. He thought she was strong? A warm feeling bloomed in her chest. And he'd demonstrated a tiny smidgen of empathy for her situation, instead of fussing at her for being clumsy.

A few minutes later, fitted with her new walking boot, she hobbled down the hall with her paperwork. Once she'd checked out, she met Heath in the waiting room.

"Hey." He stood, gesturing toward the black plastic contraption on her lower leg. "I like your boot. Black goes with everything, right?"

"Ha. Thanks, I guess." She glanced down, not at all impressed with her latest accessory. Although walking was much less painful now.

"Can I give you a ride home?"

"Yes, please." She moved slowly toward the automatic doors. When they parted and she stepped outside, a light rain was falling.

"If you don't mind waiting, I'll go get my truck and pull up closer." Heath's keys jangled in his hand. "Listen, I've been thinking. I don't want you to worry about Scout. I can make other arrangements."

"No. Scout's like the ray of sunshine in this awful storm."

Heath shot her a look. "But you're supposed to be limiting your walking, right? Besides, the fence isn't up yet. What if he takes off?"

"Maybe we can hire a teenager to help walk him. Please, Heath. I know it sounds silly, but if I'm going to sit around, Scout's good company."

Something undecipherable flickered across his features. "Okay, we'll try it. But if—"

"No buts." She linked her arms across her chest and challenged his gaze. "We had a deal. I need to uphold my half."

He scrubbed his hand across his face. "All right. We'll compromise."

She resisted the urge to punch the air with her fist. Scout made her laugh and kept her house from feeling so painfully quiet. She'd just have to be extra careful about her broken foot.

Chapter Five

He wasn't going over to her table. He wasn't going to speak to her. They happened to be in the same restaurant with different people. Not a big deal.

Heath reached for another mozzarella stick, dragged it through the pool of marinara sauce on his plate and took a bite. The crispy outside and gooey cheese combination were one of his favorite appetizers, but not much of a distraction. Because Lexi sat two tables away in a booth at Maverick's, talking and laughing with women he presumed to be her sisters. Two had the same long dark shiny hair, wide smiles and golden-brown eyes. The woman beside Lexi was taller, almost graceful, with auburn locks piled on top of her head. She looked familiar. Someone he'd seen briefly when he'd waited for Lexi at the ER last Sunday.

Conversation ebbed and flowed. Heath only half listened as one of the officers across the table regaled them all with his misadventures convincing tourists not to stop traffic while they took pictures of a mama moose with her calves. Heath hadn't responded to one of those scenarios yet. Although part of him hoped he could soon. Summer in Alaska brought about all kinds of new opportunities that he hadn't experienced working in Spokane.

A shout followed by a round of applause echoed through the dining room, drawing attention toward the darts game, where four young guys stood grinning and exchanging high fives.

Heath scanned the men and women filling the tables and huddled near the door, waiting for tables to open up. Coast Guard rescue swimmers had successfully saved two fishermen stranded at sea earlier today. Judging by the crowd, it seemed like most of Hearts Bay had wound up at Maverick's to celebrate.

"Hey, Donovan, what you staring at?" Kevin, his coworker sitting beside him at the long table, elbowed Heath in the side.

He fumbled the last of his mozzarella stick and it landed in his plate, sending a splatter of marinara onto his fleece vest.

"Nothing." Heath grabbed his napkin and dabbed at the specks.

Kevin chuckled, then tilted his head toward Lexi's table. "Do you know those ladies?"

Oh, brother.

Heath tucked the napkin under the edge of his plate, then reached for his soda. He should've stayed home tonight. A long sip of the sweet, carbonated liquid allowed him to stall before answering. He'd reluctantly joined a few of the guys from the police station. They wanted to welcome Michael, a new officer who'd just moved to town and joined the force.

He crunched on a piece of ice from his drink, weighing his words carefully. "One of them is my next-door neighbor."

It wasn't any of his business who spoke to Lexi and her sisters. He didn't have any reason not to be honest with Kevin. But something about the way the other man eyed the ladies seated at the table irritated him.

"Sweet." Kevin clapped him hard on the shoulder. "I'll need you to introduce me."

Heath bit back a snide comment. The elbowing and shoulder smacking really needed to stop.

More raucous laughter broke out on the other side of the restaurant. Heath glanced at Lexi. Her smile had dimmed. He tried not to stare. Eyes downcast, she spoke to the woman beside her. The red-haired woman eased out of the booth, and Lexi slung her purse over her shoulder, then hurried toward the back of the restaurant. An open door led to a back patio.

"I don't know her well enough to introduce her to my coworkers."

"Oh, I see how it is." Kevin's blue eyes gleamed. "You've already got a plan. Well done, my man. Well done."

"It's not like that." Heath shook his head. "She's pregnant and her husband died serving overseas. A new relationship is probably not on her radar right now."

Kevin's expression sobered. "Oh, man. That's rough."

He pushed his chair back. "Don't wait for me to order."

"Leaving already?" Kevin's brows scrunched down. "I was just joking around about meeting your neighbor. Hope I didn't offend you."

He plucked a twenty from his wallet and dropped it

on the table. "That should cover my soda and the appetizers. See you around."

Before he lost his nerve or the other guys razzed him for taking off, Heath squeezed between the tables and strode toward the women who'd been sitting with Lexi. "Excuse me. I'm sorry to interrupt. My name's Heath and Lexi's my next-door neighbor. Is she all right?"

Three sets of eyes gave him a careful once-over. He shifted awkwardly. Maybe this was a bad idea.

"It's nice to meet you, Heath. I'm Mia." The one who looked familiar extended her hand. "Are you the guy who brought her into the emergency room last weekend?"

He nodded, then shook her hand. "Yeah, we were hiking when she slipped and fell. She's tough and tried to walk it off, but I'm glad I convinced her to come see you."

"You made the right decision," Mia said, smiling.

"Thanks for looking out for her." The one sitting across from Mia smiled. "I'm Rylee Madden, one of Lexi's sisters. And this is Tess."

A woman tucked in the corner of the booth beside Rylee smiled. "Hi, Heath."

"It's nice to meet you all." Heath glanced toward the back door again. Lexi must have been standing out of sight. "Do you think she'd mind if I check on her?"

"Here." Rylee handed him a mason jar full of strawberry lemonade. "Take her drink to her. She'll appreciate that."

Really? He hesitated before accepting the drink. He was way outside his comfort zone here, but he had a feeling if he didn't go outside and speak to Lexi, some other guy in the restaurant might.

"I'll go make sure she's feeling well." He snatched a napkin off the table. The glow from more curious gazes warmed his skin as he worked his way toward the back door. After his brief conversation with Kevin, he felt compelled to protect Lexi from one of the many flirtatious dudes hanging out at Maverick's tonight. He'd bring her the lemonade, make sure she was okay, and then he'd leave her be. He was just being neighborly.

She needed to pull herself together.

Lexi stood outside Maverick's on the spacious fenced-in patio, her back to the restaurant. When would she stop tearing up at every little thing? She fanned her fingers in front of her face. A pleasant breeze swirled around her, rippling the fabric of her dress against her bare legs. An aroma of burgers and French fries filled the air. Her stomach growled. She pressed her hand to her abdomen.

"I know, baby. Give me a minute," she whispered, an involuntary shiver tiptoeing across her shoulders. Grateful for the denim jacket she'd slipped on at the last minute, Lexi leaned against the plastic picket-style fence. So strange how one minute she was perfectly happy, enjoying her strawberry lemonade and great conversation with Tess, Mia and Rylee. Then she'd spotted men in their Coast Guard uniforms, slapping backs and bumping fists, and a gaping hole reopened in her heart.

She missed her friends back home. The family she'd grown up with. Beau. He wasn't even in the Coast Guard, but seeing the guys celebrating together and playing darts had dredged up the hurt.

"C'mon, girl. Quit feeling sorry for yourself." Beau was gone. There was nothing she could do. But no matter how hard she tried, she couldn't will the grief away.

She pressed her fingertip delicately to the corner of each eye, hoping to stanch the tears.

Children squealed. Two preschool boys scampered around the tiny play structure on the restaurant's back patio. A young couple stood nearby, smiling. The man had his arm around the woman's shoulders as she used her phone to take a picture of her toddler enjoying the baby swing.

An irrational pang of envy knifed through her. She turned away and faced the street.

Maybe she should go home. Except she'd ridden with Rylee, and she didn't want to make her leave early. Besides, they hadn't received the food they'd ordered yet. She could do this. Lexi squared her shoulders. She could go back in there, pretend the close-knit community and the camaraderie of the guys having a good time together didn't bother her.

Except Heath was in there, too. They'd locked eyes at least twice since she'd sat down in the booth near his table. He and his friends seemed to be enjoying some appetizers. No matter how hard she'd focused her attention on her sisters, against her will, her gaze kept sliding toward her neighbor.

"Are you all right?"

She turned at the sound of Heath's voice. He stood a few feet away, holding a glass of strawberry lemonade and a napkin. In hiking boots, stone-colored cargo pants, a long-sleeved white shirt and a navy blue fleece vest, he looked like he'd returned from an expedition.

"Did Rylee send you out here?"

"No. I saw you leave. To be honest, there's a guy at my table asking about you, and I didn't want him to come out here and start…" He trailed off, pink tinge-ing his cheeks.

"And start what?"

His Adam's apple bobbed. He looked everywhere but at her. "I was concerned he would ask you out and you wouldn't want that."

Oh. She couldn't stop a smile. "Thank you."

"Here." He held out the napkin and the lemonade.

She took the glass and the napkin, her fingers brush-ing against his. A pleasant sensation zipped along her arm. He jammed his hands in his front pockets, then sidestepped the two little boys chasing each other.

"It's very sweet of you to look out for me."

His gaze slid to meet hers. Concern flickered in his eyes. He lifted one shoulder. "Just trying to do the right thing."

She discreetly dabbed at the moisture lingering on her cheeks, then took a sip of her lemonade. "You don't have to stand out here with me."

He glanced over his shoulder. "Oh, I think I should."

"Why? Is your friend not a nice person?"

"We've only worked together for a few weeks. Seems like a decent guy. We're here because our department hired a new police officer. Trying to make him feel welcome."

She studied him over the rim of her glass. "That sounds fun."

"Not really."

"Can I ask you a favor, then?" she murmured.

"Sure."

"Do you think you could drive me home?"

His mouth tipped up in a half smile. "Absolutely."

"Thanks." She paused, not wanting to go into much detail about her melancholy mood.

A few minutes later, she'd dropped her glass off at her table, explained she'd prefer to go home and followed Heath out to his truck.

"Is there anything I can do to help get your camera repaired?"

She shook her head. "I appreciate the offer, but I already paid an arm and a leg to Express Mail it to a repair shop in Anchorage."

He unlocked his truck and opened the passenger door for her. "The festival is only two weeks from today. Will you have the camera back by then?"

She maneuvered into the passenger seat. "Hope so."

He gently closed the door.

Lexi smoothed her hands over the fabric of her dress, then set her purse on the floorboards. Her foot hurt. This was day six of wearing the boot and walking had been cumbersome. She settled back against the seat, grateful Heath had come to her rescue. Again.

She forced herself not to stare as he circled around the front of the truck, opened his door and climbed inside.

"One more thing." He put the key in the ignition. "We need to talk about your plans for Fish Fest. The delay with my fence has me concerned about getting you what you'll need for your booth. If I have to special order anything, the folks at the hardware store mentioned I should allow for extra time."

"Okay, so don't laugh." She rubbed her palms together as she twisted to face him. "This might sound cheesy, but I want to do one of those booths where people pose with their heads in the cutout and there's some cute phrase and a themed outfit painted on the plywood. Wouldn't that be fun?"

"Have you seen the pictures posted on the Town of Hearts Bay website?"

"No. Why? Is somebody already doing that?"

Heath shook his head. "Not that I know of, but there's a local artist who designed what you're describing for a couple who had a wedding here recently. Wonder if you could borrow the props?"

She sucked in a breath and pressed her hand to his arm. "Heath, you're brilliant. That's a fantastic idea!"

His gaze slid from her face to her hand still lingering on his arm.

Warmth flushed her cheeks and she pulled away, trying to hide her embarrassment by grabbing her phone from her purse. "I'm going to look at the website right now and get the artist's name."

Heath started the truck. "I'll drive you home."

She scrolled to the web page he'd mentioned but she couldn't focus. He was being so kind, replacing the flowers Scout had ruined, taking her to the ER when she'd been clumsy on their hike. And all she was doing in return was hanging out with Scout.

Did he want to be more than neighbors and friends?

She sneaked a glance from the corner of her eye. Heath drove with both hands on the wheel, staring straight ahead. There hadn't been an ounce of flirtation in his words or his actions.

He'd even said his work as a police officer required him to be helpful.

Honestly, you're totally overthinking this. Clearly she was in over her head with her dumb foot fracture, which had provided him with ample opportunities to assist her.

That was all this was.

Pursing her lips, she continued to study him. Yeah, okay, so maybe the air in the truck crackled a little when they were together. She'd made him smile a time or two. But that didn't mean anything. He'd even admitted that he'd brought her lemonade on the patio so that the other guys at the table didn't flirt with her.

Being a decent human didn't mean he was interested. Right?

"What do you mean he got fired?"

Heath eased into the chair at his kitchen table, the phone pressed to his ear.

Mom sighed. "Reid didn't want me to tell you, but he'd fallen asleep a few times in the break room. Yesterday he bungled an order when he was using the forklift—"

"Bungled an order how?"

Scout left his dog bed, ambled over and rested his snout on Heath's leg. He raked his fingers through the dog's curly hair on top of his big head, grateful for the small comfort of the animal's presence.

"He knocked over a pallet in the warehouse and they lost some product because it was damaged."

Oh, no. Heath squeezed his eyes shut. "Has he been to the doctor?"

"Not yet."

He opened his eyes and resumed petting Scout. The dog sat down, leaning his body against Heath's leg. "What's Reid going to do now?"

"Right now he's outside mowing my lawn like it's a golf course at the country club."

"Then he must not be too exhausted. Maybe this was just a fluke?"

"It's possible. Although he did say that he'd received two warnings. Since he refuses to go to the doctor or get any genetic testing done, he can't ask his employer for accommodations."

A hollow ache filled his stomach. "Mom, do you think Reid has Huntington's?"

"Sweetheart, that's not for me to say. There are some similarities between Reid and your dad's condition when he was Reid's age. But you know how your brother is. He doesn't want to talk about it."

Heath couldn't blame him. Huntington's disease, the onset of symptoms and the possibility of being a carrier were topics he tried to avoid, too. But other than being exhausted after a demanding shift sometimes, he wasn't struggling with symptoms that impacted his performance at work.

"I'm sorry that Reid lost his job and that you have to go through this," he said. "What can I do?"

"You can pray."

Um, not the first action item on his to-do list. Heath pressed his lips together to keep from saying something stupid.

"Please pray that if Reid has a life-changing disease, he'll have the courage to get help and let me take care of him."

"Mom, no. You don't have to be his caregiver."

"He's my son and your brother. Since he's single, what am I supposed to do? Make him suffer in isolation?"

"Of course not." Heath tipped his head back and stared at the ceiling. Guilt slid in, making him feel like a jerk for implying that Reid should figure this out on his own. "I'm sorry. That's not what I meant."

He stopped short of voicing his greatest fear. That his mother might have to go through what she went through caring for Dad.

Scout whined, then licked Heath's hand. He looked down. The animal's soulful eyes were locked on his. Heath scratched behind Scout's ears. Just touching the dog and having him close by loosened the tension squeezing his lungs.

"I know Reid won't call or text you to let you know what's going on." Mom sniffed.

He winced. Was she crying? Maybe he should reach out to his brother. But Mom was right. Reid wouldn't be into that at all. Still, that whole suffering-in-silence thing wasn't fair, either.

"And I apologize if I put you in an awkward spot, but I had to talk to someone I could trust," she said.

"You can call me anytime. I want to know what's going on, even if there's nothing I can do."

"Prayer is a powerful force, Heath. You can always talk to the Lord."

"I know." He hesitated. "I'll try."

He hadn't prayed at all lately. Or made the effort to find a church in Hearts Bay to attend. Or done anything, really, to work on his relationship with God. Because he was still so angry. And now, hearing the news that Reid might have the same disease that took their father from them didn't make Heath real eager to ask the Lord to intervene. But he couldn't pretend that this wasn't happening. Mom had asked him to pray, so he would.

Outside the house, a car door slammed. Scout sprinted toward the door, his bark echoing through the house.

"I've got to go." Heath stood. "I'm having a fence installed and the contractor's here."

"I need to run, too. Reid's coming inside. I'll talk to you soon, sweetie."

He ended the call and set the phone on the table.

The doorbell rang, prompting Scout to bark even louder. Heath crossed the room, pausing as he spotted Lexi through his living room window in her backyard, watering flowers.

Part of him hoped she'd still be outside when he went into the backyard with the contractor. His thoughts turned to Lexi often. He found himself mentally making lists of things he wanted to share. This sobering news from his mother about Reid topped that list.

But he couldn't. There was no way he'd share his concerns about his family's health history. It wasn't fair to pile that burden on Lexi. She already had a daunting future ahead as a single mom-to-be. So as much as he longed to talk to someone about Reid, Lexi couldn't be that person.

Chapter Six

"These are great." Mackenzie Jackson scrolled through the photos Lexi had uploaded from her camera's memory card and her phone and transferred to her laptop. The hike on the Mount Larsen trail hadn't been a complete debacle after all.

"Thanks." Lexi refilled her friend's glass of lemonade. "I wish I hadn't damaged my camera and broken my foot. The scenery is incredible. I can't wait to take more pictures."

"Have you considered teaching a digital course?"

She furrowed her brow. "A digital what?"

"You know, an online class. Don't you ever get those ads on social media? People teach a ton of different classes online now. Everything from how to declutter your house to getting little kids to eat well." Mackenzie stopped scrolling and smiled. "You could show folks how to take beautiful photos."

Lexi set the lemonade pitcher on the table, then pulled out a chair and sat down. "I'm not sure I should take on any other projects right now."

Mackenzie studied her, doubt flickering in her bright

blue eyes. "You strike me as the kind of woman who can do anything you put your mind to."

"That's sweet of you to say." Lexi fidgeted with the hem of her menswear-style pin-striped tunic, wishing she hadn't dressed so basic. The remnants of Scout's hair on her black leggings wasn't all that cool, either.

After her visit with Dr. Rasmussen yesterday had confirmed she'd gained seven pounds, she felt quite frumpy. Especially sitting next to Mackenzie and her pulled-together look.

"All right. No pressure." Mackenzie scrolled through the photos on the screen again. "But I just think you're very talented and people would love to learn from you."

"Thank you again for the suggestion. I'll keep it in mind. To be honest, I wouldn't even know how to get started."

"Well, there's an online course for that, too." Mackenzie laughed. "If you change your mind, let me know. I can probably help you figure out how to get started."

"Do you teach any— What did you call it? Digital courses?"

Lexi eyed the plate of oatmeal chocolate chip cookies she'd set out for them to nibble on but resisted the urge to reach for one. She grabbed a handful of mini-pretzels instead.

"No, not yet. But the blog is my first step. I need something to keep me focused when I'm not taking care of the kids. My husband's gone a lot."

Mackenzie's comment made Lexi's breath catch. Her pretzel lodged in her throat and she coughed.

"Oh, no." Mackenzie clapped her hand to her mouth, eyes wide.

Lexi stopped coughing, reached for her lemonade and took a sip. The tart drink was cold but didn't soothe the ache in her throat.

"I'm so sorry," Mackenzie said. "That was incredibly insensitive."

Lexi waved a dismissive hand. "It's okay. You can be honest. I know what it's like to have a spouse deployed."

"But I shouldn't be whining to you about my husband working long hours."

"It's fine. C'mon—let me show you something." Lexi stood and motioned for her friend to follow her. "There's an artist here in town who painted some adorable photo props for a wedding. She said it was a wedding gift for the bride and groom. Anyway, I asked to borrow them and now they're in my garage."

"Oh, how fun. Let's see them." Mackenzie trailed Lexi down the short hallway to the garage. They sidestepped one of Scout's toys lying on the floor. "I didn't know you had a dog," she said.

"I don't." Lexi opened the door and flicked the light switch on. "I've been dog sitting for the guy who lives next door. He's back in his crate at my neighbor's house right now."

Thankfully, Mackenzie spotted the photo-booth props and saved Lexi from answering any more questions about her dog-sitting arrangement with Heath. He and Asher had leaned the plywood against the far wall.

"Here, I'll put the door up, and we can get a better look." Lexi tapped the button and the motor hummed as it retracted the garage door. They scooted around her car.

"Wow! These are so clever." Mackenzie ran her hand

over the first one. It featured cutouts for four faces. The artist had designed and painted four adorable outfits to match each cutout. Perfect for a family who wanted a fishing-themed photo op. The next prop had been custom-made for two people on a hike, complete with illustrations of a bear, a moose and some squirrels in the background. The third photo prop was designed specifically for two people on the bow of a boat with a scenic mountain and ocean background.

"Do you think this will work for a Fish Fest photo booth?" Lexi pressed her palms to her lower back and tried to stand in a way that took the pressure off her injured foot.

"Absolutely. People are going to love this." Mackenzie's eyes sparkled as she clasped her hands. "Now, do you have a plan in place to collect email addresses? Or give them a promo code for a discount off your fall mini sessions?"

A promo code? Lexi frowned. "I hadn't thought that far ahead. If my camera doesn't get repaired, I won't be able to do any photo sessions at all."

"Let's stay positive, okay? Fish Fest is coming up quick. There's a printing service on the island, if you want to hand out flyers. Or if you collected their email addresses, you could email them a promo code for a discount on a future photo session. After you take a picture for them at Fish Fest using these amazing props, make sure you get their email address, then send a message a day or two later, encouraging them to book a holiday mini session and save money with your exclusive promo code. Make sense?"

Lexi's head spun at all that needed to be done to

bring this email marketing opportunity to fruition. But she couldn't back out now.

"I need to go in a few minutes." Mackenzie glanced at her phone. "By the way, how did you get this in here?"

"Heath, my next-door neighbor, and my brother-in-law moved them for me."

"I've heard about your next-door neighbor," Mackenzie teased.

Lexi stifled a groan and jabbed at the button to lower the garage door. "What have you heard?"

"That he's cute and the two of you have been spending a lot of time together."

"Stop it." Lexi followed Mackenzie to the table. "People are seriously talking about us?"

"Yep." She grinned. "That's what happens when half the Coast Guard base sees you leaving Maverick's together."

"Oh, no." Lexi couldn't stifle her groan this time. "In case y'all haven't noticed, I'm expecting."

"So?"

"So I wouldn't expect a guy to date me knowing I'm going to have a newborn by Christmas."

Mackenzie pulled her keys from her purse. "He's not married and you're single, right?"

"But it's complicated."

"What's complicated about falling in love with your next-door neighbor?" She sighed. "Talk about totally adorable. It would make such a great movie."

"Ha, that's cute. Except my life is anything but a feel-good romance movie."

"You never know what can happen, especially if you keep dog sitting." Mackenzie winked, then shouldered her purse. "Let's talk soon."

After she walked her friend to the door, Lexi emailed her three pictures of the waterfall that she'd taken, and a couple more of Mount Larsen and the bald eagle flying overhead. Mackenzie had already promised to link back to Lexi's website, as well as tag her in the photos on social media.

Lexi cleaned up the lemonade, cookies and pretzels. Mackenzie's advice about teaching an online course and her comments about falling in love with her neighbor spooled through her head. Yeah, she should probably be more intentional about growing her business. But all she could think about was Heath. Mackenzie had been right. They were single and neighbors, and he was most definitely cute. Not to mention thoughtful and protective and a true gentleman.

But Beau hadn't been gone all that long. And in less than five months all of her attention would be devoted to her newborn. She didn't want to be single forever, but it was far too soon to think about dating someone.

Heath had never been this thrilled to run an errand for a neighbor.

Lexi's request had arrived at just the right time. He'd been on his way home from work when she'd sent a text asking him to pick up her camera. It had arrived from Anchorage on the afternoon flight.

Heath parked his truck in his driveway and climbed out. With only two days until Fish Fest and nothing but glorious sunshine in the forecast, Orca Island was abuzz with excitement. Tourists seemed friendlier, and locals rushed around like worker bees taking care of last-minute preparations. Even his coworker Kevin had agreed to trade shifts with him so Heath could take Saturday off and help Lexi prep her booth for the festival.

Sunlight warmed his skin and spilled across the lush green lawn. Kids from the neighborhood shouted to one another as they rode their bikes up and down the street. Heath left his backpack in the truck and crossed the yard to Lexi's place, the package with her repaired camera inside tucked protectively against his chest.

He stopped to examine his partially finished fence. Movement from the corner of his eye and a familiar bark caught his attention. He turned around. Lexi had tethered Scout on a long line in her backyard. She stood near the edge of her property that she shared with the house behind hers, picking something from the green bushes and putting it in a white plastic bucket.

"Hey." She smiled and his heart drummed against his ribs. "Is that my camera?"

Scout barked again and lunged, his pink tongue lolling.

"I think so. Hey, buddy." Heath stopped in the middle of the yard. Scout jumped and pressed his paws against Heath's chest. "Whoa. Easy there. *Sit.*"

The dog whined, then sank back on his haunches. He kept panting, the tuft of curls on top of his head fluttering in the late-afternoon breeze. Heath gave him a quick pat, then continued across the yard. He stopped beside Lexi.

She'd piled her dark hair on top of her head in a bun. How did women do that? He'd never understand. Her short-sleeved red, white and blue flowered shirt and denim shorts hinted at the growing baby she carried. A healthy glow highlighted her cheeks.

"Raspberry?" She'd painted her nails a new shade

of light blue, which he couldn't help but notice when she held out the bucket.

"Hey, where's your boot?"

Her eyebrows scrunched together. "I had to take it off. The fabric inside makes my leg itch so bad. Look." She pointed to her bare leg. A red splotchy rash marred the skin above her ankle.

"Ouch. I see your point." Heath dragged his gaze to meet hers. "But shouldn't you at least be sitting down with your foot elevated?"

"Don't worry. Mia gave me special permission to take it off. I promise I'll sit down and prop my foot up right after I pick these berries. They're so good." She tilted the bucket his way. "You have to try one."

He selected one raspberry and tried not to grimace. He'd never been a fan of the fuzzy, bumpy texture.

"Don't make that face. Come on. It won't hurt you, I promise."

Reluctantly, he popped it in his mouth. The sweet, juicy, sun-drenched flavor was a nice surprise.

"See?" Lexi's whole face lit up. "Do you want more?"

He leaned closer and peered into the container. "Are you sure you want to share? There aren't very many in here. Are you eating more than you pick?"

"Shhh," she said in a mock whisper. "Don't tell."

"Are you planning to make something with these?"

"I had hoped to pick enough to make jam. The Madden sisters have a legendary recipe, but at the rate I'm going, I'll only have enough berries to make a batch of muffins."

"Nothing wrong with muffins."

Scout barked, drawing a laugh from Lexi.

Man, he could get used to hearing that.

"This is fun," Lexi said, plucking another berry from the bush. "And I feel a bit more like an Alaskan out here picking berries in August."

"So Alaskans pick berries in August?"

"When they're not fishing or celebrating fishing."

Scout barked again.

Lexi gave the dog a look. "He wants you to see his collection of sticks."

No, thanks. Couldn't care less. Not with Lexi standing beside him looking more beautiful than ever. He shook off the thought and turned to look at his obnoxious dog.

"I tethered him to the stake because I didn't want him to run away." She gestured toward her foot. "Since I'm not in any shape to chase him. We haven't been out here for more than twenty minutes, but he's managed to drag about six different sticks out of these bushes."

"Thanks for keeping him entertained. My fence should be finished by next week. Then he can play in his own yard."

"Oh, now, where's the fun in that?" she teased. "I love having him around. He's a great dog."

"You've been good for him." Heath carefully set the package at his feet, then yanked a stick from the bushes nearby and gently tossed it toward Scout. "He's so tired that he can't misbehave by the time I get home."

Scout pounced, grabbed the stick and held it proudly, his nose thrust toward the sky.

Heath shook his head. "What a goofball."

Lexi dropped a few more raspberries into her bucket. "I brought more appropriate toys out here, I promise."

"Maybe he dug a hole and buried them."

"What? No." Lexi whirled around. "He wouldn't do that."

Heath laughed. "Just kidding. No worries. He seems quite happy with another stick." They both reached to pluck a raspberry off a bush at the same time and their fingers brushed together. Scout's jaws working on the stick, the kids playing, a lawn mower humming nearby—all of it faded into the background. He didn't want to move. Didn't want to pull away.

Lexi stared up at him. How had he not noticed the appealing fringe of her dark eyelashes? Or the specks of gold ringing the dark irises? They stood incredibly close. The air crackled between them.

He reached up and gently slid the pad of his thumb across her cheek. "You have raspberry juice on your cheek."

"Do I?" Her voice was barely above a whisper. She blanketed his hand with hers, keeping his palm cupped against her jaw. Her soft skin and the warmth of her touch made his rowdy heart trip out a frantic beat.

He managed a nod. Her warm gaze surveyed his face. Was she leaning closer? Maybe he'd imagined that.

It took everything in him not to close the last of the distance between them and kiss her.

Before he could take a step back, Lexi pressed up on her toes and brushed her lips against his. He closed his eyes and tilted his head. Her mouth tasted sweet from the raspberries and he couldn't help himself. He had to keep kissing her. She let her hand travel up his arm and gently gripped his shoulder. He cradled the back of her head with his palm. The berry bucket slipped from her hand and landed with a *thunk* on the ground.

She didn't seem to care. Lacing her fingers behind his neck, she let him deepen the kiss.

She hadn't meant to kiss him. But he'd looked so handsome standing there in uniform, clearly only eating a raspberry because she'd convinced him to try it. Then he'd touched her cheek and she'd about melted. With his mouth moving against hers, and his hand cradling the back of her head like she was the most precious thing in the world, she'd nearly forgotten that she was a widowed mom-to-be.

A strange flutter in her abdomen, a sensation she'd never experienced before, tugged her back to reality.

Oh, no. She unlaced her fingers from the nape of Heath's neck and stepped away, her chest heaving. "What have I done?"

Pain flashed in Heath's eyes. He smoothed his palm over the top of his head. "You didn't do anything wrong, Lexi."

His voice sounded gravelly.

"I'm so sorry." She sidestepped the bucket on the ground, wincing as she put pressure on her healing foot and took a few steps away.

She limped toward her back patio. Scout stood and trotted toward her. The rope on his tether allowed him to get close enough to lick her hand. She pressed her palm to the top of his soft head. He sat down and leaned against her leg.

She forced herself to meet Heath's gaze. "I'm really sorry. I—I shouldn't have kissed you."

A host of emotions crisscrossed his face. "Why do you keep apologizing? I kissed you back."

And, oh, what a kiss. Warmth still bloomed on her

skin from his touch. "But kissing wasn't really part of our...arrangement."

His features drew tight. "I never expected you to kiss me because I ran an errand for you."

Argh, this was awkward. She pressed her fist to her forehead. "Look. Here's the thing. I'm not ready for a relationship. Beau's only been gone a few months and I've got a baby coming. Thank you for all the help you've given me, and kissing you was amazing, but I just need to—"

He held up both palms. "I get it. You don't have to say anything more."

"Thank you for understanding."

Heath picked up the box and brought it to her. "Here's your camera. I'll be by early Saturday morning to help you get to the festival."

She nodded, and then she took the package and hurried away as fast as her sore foot would allow. Scout barked and whined, but she didn't turn back. Inside, she set the box containing her repaired camera on the kitchen counter and headed straight for the freezer. Forget dinner. This called for a serious amount of ice cream. Maybe syrup, whipped cream and sprinkles, too.

Why had she been so bold and initiated a kiss?

One minute they were talking about raspberries and Scout's antics, and the next she'd planted one on him like she didn't have a care in the world. More of that strange fluttering sensation in her stomach caught her attention. She set the pint of ice cream down and stood still.

It happened again. A subtle movement. Like someone was...

She gasped and pressed her palm to her taut stomach. Her baby had moved enough for her to feel the activity.

Lexi didn't bother to even try to stop the tears. Another milestone in her journey as a mother and there was no one here to experience the moment with her. There was no way she'd tell Heath now. Or ask him to come back over. Not after she'd kissed him and then said it shouldn't have happened.

"It's just you and me, little one." She patted her tummy one more time. "We've got to figure this out together."

Pulling a tissue from the box nearby, she mopped up her tears, then popped the lid off the container of chocolate peanut butter swirl. Her sisters had made sure her freezer was stocked with plenty of meals and ice cream. This particular flavor would probably keep her awake. But that didn't matter. She'd be tossing and turning anyway. Trying not to think about how Heath's tender touch had stolen her breath. Or the look in his eyes when she'd apologized. Twice.

She groaned as she dug through the drawer to find the ice cream scoop. Had she done the right thing? Or been incredibly cruel? Friendship was best at this point, wasn't it? She had to prepare for her baby's arrival. Mentally, physically and emotionally. Motherhood was supposed to be her focus. Well, that and padding her savings account. She couldn't leap into a brand-new relationship. That wasn't fair to Heath. From now on, anyone she dated would have to be willing to be a part of her child's life, too.

Her phone hummed with an incoming text. She ignored it and scooped a generous portion of chocolate peanut butter swirl into the bowl, then added whipped cream and rainbow sprinkles. As much as she wanted to share her news that her baby had moved, she wasn't in any shape to communicate with anyone right now.

Bowl of ice cream in hand, Lexi relocated to the living room. As she passed the framed photo of her and Beau on the table, guilt pinched her insides. Goodness, her emotions were tangled like the strands of Christmas lights she'd pulled from storage boxes every holiday season. She heaved a sigh and settled on the sofa. If only Scout was here, snuggled up at her feet, keeping her company. Ready and willing to listen to her sort through her feelings out loud.

"Don't be ridiculous," she whispered, reaching for the remote control. "You don't need to borrow Heath's dog for emotional support."

She turned on the TV, scrolled to an episode of *Gilmore Girls* and propped her foot up on the coffee table. Sadly, the first bite of cold, decadent ice cream loaded with whipped cream and sprinkles offered little comfort. She still felt guilty. Guilty for kissing Heath. Guilty for being attracted to someone new when Beau had only recently passed away. Once again, her impulsiveness had brought on a heap of trouble. No matter how handsome or kind Heath had been, or how much she adored Scout, kissing Heath had been a huge mistake.

Chapter Seven

Early Saturday morning, Heath stood on his back patio, a tendril of steam curling from the mug of coffee he held in his hand. The scent of sawdust and cedar lingered in the air. Scout bounded happily along the picket-style fence framing half the yard, tail wagging as he sniffed the ground. Hopefully by this time next week, the contractor would have the fence completed. Not that the firm boundary around his property was guaranteed to keep Scout contained. The dog adored spending time with Lexi. Something told Heath that Scout would still find a way to get next door.

He couldn't fault the mischievous animal one bit.

Heath discreetly glanced toward her house. No sign that she was up yet. Although probably few people were awake. The clock on his coffee maker had indicated it was just before 6:00 a.m. Fish Fest didn't start for another two hours, but he hadn't been able to sleep.

Thoughts of Lexi, that kiss and the look of sheer regret in her eyes had been on his mind frequently for the last two days.

When he was driving, his traitorous thoughts returned to Lexi's soft skin under his fingertips. He'd been caught zoning out in a meeting with the police chief yesterday. However, traffic detours for the festival were the least of his worries, especially since he'd traded shifts with Kevin. All Heath had wanted to rehash was the warmth of Lexi's kiss.

He took a cautious sip of his coffee and tried not to look toward the raspberry bushes in her backyard. That would just provoke another instant replay of their entire interaction. Including the spectacularly painful conclusion.

It still hurt to admit, but Lexi had been right. They shouldn't have allowed themselves to get lost in the moment. Sure, she'd initiated the kiss, but he'd been a willing participant. And he hadn't done a thing to stop her when she'd moved closer.

He had no business kissing her. Not when she'd lost her husband a few months ago and she had a baby coming before Christmas. Besides, nothing had changed about his own complicated genetic history. If he carried a defective gene, there was a 50 percent chance he'd pass Huntington's on if he had children of his own. That was the deal breaker. Conveniently, he'd forgotten all of that when he'd had his lips on hers.

But today the truth was painfully clear. He needed to double down. Regroup. He had lost his head for a minute and foolishly believed that a future with Lexi and her child was a possibility.

He whistled for Scout. The dog complied and trotted toward him. How about that. For once Scout didn't dart in the opposite direction. They went inside the house. Heath set his mug on the counter, then filled Scout's food and water bowls.

The dog chowed down and Heath fixed himself a bowl of oatmeal. By the time he'd finished eating, showered and played a quick game of fetch with Scout, he spotted Asher Hale pulling into Lexi's driveway.

Heath coaxed Scout into his crate with a tasty dog treat, then went outside.

"Good morning." Asher waved and opened the tailgate of his truck.

"Good morning," Heath said, crossing the narrow strip of grass between his and Lexi's yard. "Thanks for helping me load these props."

"No problem." Asher pulled his phone from his back pocket. "Lexi sent me a text with the code to open her garage door, just in case she wasn't awake yet."

Heath waited for Asher to input the numbers in the keypad. The sun had been up for a couple of hours already. Its pale golden rays made the dew on the grass sparkle. Wisps of fog still clung to the mountains. A flawless baby blue sky stretched overhead. They couldn't have asked for a more perfect day.

Lexi's garage door rattled and hummed as it retracted.

"Do you want to wear gloves?" Asher gestured to his truck. "I brought three pairs."

"Yes, please."

Heath tugged on the pair Asher offered him. Then they went into the garage and carefully transported the finished photo-booth props to Asher's truck. Heath grunted, his muscles straining, as they slid the first one into the truck's bed. Maybe they should've found an additional person to help. The plywood frames were cumbersome. There wasn't much time to spare, though. They needed to get over to Fish Fest and make sure Lexi had everything she needed before the rest of the town descended. And to be honest, he needed to prepare himself for seeing her for the first time since they'd kissed.

Yesterday, he had texted that he'd make other arrangements for Scout since Lexi had last-minute prep for the festival. Then he'd taken Scout to a new dog sitter he'd found through a social media ad. The lady had done a decent job, but Scout had been kind of mopey on the ride home afterward. When Heath had let him out of the truck, Scout had sprinted to Lexi's doorstep. It had taken three treats and a dollop of peanut butter to get the dog back inside his own house.

"Looks like we're all set." Asher eyed him after they'd loaded the last prop. "Rylee's coming by to pick Lexi up and drive her to the festival."

Heath took off the gloves and gave them back. "Sounds good."

But Rylee serving as Lexi's driver didn't really sound good to him. Not at all. He wanted to be that guy. Hopefully his face didn't hint at his disappointment. Had Lexi told her sisters what had happened between them? Surely the news hadn't reached Asher yet. Heath barely knew the guy. He wasn't about to pour his heart out. Lexi catching a ride with someone else was probably for the best. But that didn't mean he had to like it.

Heath hovered in the driveway, hoping Lexi might come outside and say hello. Or thank them for helping her prepare for the festival. But to his disappointment, the lights weren't on and the door leading from the garage to the house remained closed.

"Thanks for helping out." Asher jabbed the buttons

on the keypad. The garage door rolled down. "I'll see you at the festival."

"See ya." Heath waited until Asher drove away, then headed for his own truck.

He'd toyed with the idea of bringing Scout to the festival, but he couldn't manage the dog *and* setting up the booth. Maybe he'd come back later and pick up Scout. The Goldendoodle needed the experience of being around a crowd, and Heath needed canine companionship. A source of comfort and loyalty to get through what would likely be an awkward day.

A few minutes later, he found a parking spot designated for volunteers not far from Town Hall. Asher must've found a way to get his truck closer to the booth's staging area, because Heath didn't see him. Hopefully they'd be able to arrange the props before Lexi got there. Anything he could do to make her life easier today and ensure that she didn't put too much stress on her foot, he'd do.

People milled about, chatting as they unfolded tables and hung up decorations. A banner proclaiming Hearts Bay's Fifteenth Annual Fish Fest hung between two streetlights in the middle of Main Street. Lexi had been assigned a booth not far from The Trading Post coffee shop.

Heath couldn't help but smile. Proximity to the source of her favorite beverage would make her happy. Traffic had already been rerouted to keep vehicles off Main Street. The administrative assistant who worked at the police station had told him they estimated over seventy-five vendors had signed up to run booths. The aroma of something sweet hung in the air, hinting at the treats that would be available soon.

Asher waved him down, then motioned to his truck, positioned to unload. Heath jogged toward him. He could do this. For Lexi. He could forget that kiss, put aside his feelings of romantic attraction and be the friend that she needed him to be.

Her foot hurt, her back ached and she needed something to drink. But she still had at least ten families waiting in line to get their pictures taken. So she wasn't about to stop or turn them away. The weather for the festival had cooperated. Not a drop of rain had fallen. A subtle layer of clouds had rolled in after lunch. She missed the warmth from the sun, but the slightly overcast sky kept people from having to squint at her camera. Her recently repaired, good-as-new camera.

Thank You, Lord, for Your perfect timing, she silently prayed.

The photo props were a huge hit. So far, most of the local residents who'd stopped and posed for pictures had signed up for her email newsletter list and taken a coupon to use later for her fall photo sessions.

And to think she'd initially rejected Mackenzie's marketing tips. What a mistake that would've been. When Mackenzie and her family had stopped by, Lexi had thanked her profusely. Later, she'd buy all four of them a gift certificate for a nice dinner out.

A young couple standing at the front of the line stepped forward, holding hands. He wore a plaid button-down layered over a T-shirt, jeans and hiking boots. The woman wore a long-sleeved white shirt, pink vest, jeans and sneakers. They exchanged knowing smiles like there wasn't another human for miles around.

How adorable. Lexi waited for them to step behind the plywood props.

Instead, the guy dropped to one knee and reached for the woman's hand.

Oh, my. A collective gasp went up from the on-lookers. Adrenaline surged through Lexi's veins. She couldn't miss this. She deftly lifted her camera to capture the moment.

The woman's eyes filled with tears and she pressed one hand to her mouth.

From his stance kneeling on one knee, the guy reached for her left hand, then produced a ring from his pocket somehow and offered a sweet, simple proposal.

Tears pricked Lexi's eyes but she willed them away. This wasn't the time to get distracted by her own emotions. She had one opportunity to get these shots.

"Yes, I'll marry you." The woman smiled through her tears and Lexi orbited around them. Her boot *thunk-thunk-thunked* on the asphalt.

She groaned inwardly. Had she ruined the moment? She wasn't exactly being discreet. But the man had chosen to propose in the middle of a crowded festival. Her camera clicked and whirred as she took another photo of the man and woman kissing. Then they embraced and applause broke out.

When the couple parted, their smiles were priceless and Lexi snapped another quick picture. "Congratulations, y'all. That was amazing! Would you like me to take more pictures?"

Who knew that one festival photo booth would lead to an impromptu marriage proposal?

"Sure! And do you have a business card?" the newly-engaged woman asked. "I'd love to connect with you later about purchasing some of those photos. We're visiting from Fairbanks."

"Here." Lexi handed them a flyer from her table, then snapped a few more shots of the happy couple. "Thanks for coming to Fish Fest. I doubt you'll be back for my fall photo session, but the same rates will apply if you choose to purchase a package. Here's all the information you need, including my website address and contact info."

"Thank you so much," the guy said. "I didn't plan on proposing right here, but I couldn't help myself."

"I'm glad I could be a small part of your special day," Lexi said. "Congrats again."

"Thank you." They walked away, still holding hands. Lexi watched them go. So sweet.

"Do you need to sit down for a minute?"

Heath's familiar voice caused her to turn around.

He stood with a hand on a folding chair behind her table. Scout sat down beside the chair, whining softly. Heath kept the dog's leash wrapped around his forearm.

"I'm okay for now." Lexi glanced toward the people still waiting in line. They seemed genuinely thrilled that they'd witnessed a marriage proposal, but she didn't expect their patience to last much longer.

A muscle in Heath's cheek twitched.

"Let me finish taking these pictures and then I'll take a break."

His piercing gaze stayed locked on hers.

Clearly he didn't approve of her decision, but she wasn't about to disappoint these folks and risk losing future customers. Two young girls standing near the end of the line spotted Scout and rushed over, squealing.

Heath's eyes grew wide. Lexi pressed her lips together to conceal her amusement. Maybe having Scout here would provide a bonus. A nice distraction. The children were only about five or six. They patted his soft curls and asked Heath several questions, which he answered with brief responses.

Scout sat proudly, his eyes gleaming. Fluffy tail swishing. More kids surrounded him. Lexi couldn't resist snapping a couple of photos. How could one four-legged animal be such a star attraction? She didn't know. But she wasn't about to complain, either.

"All right, friends." She turned to the family of four who'd posed behind the plywood and poked their heads through the openings. "Look at the camera and say, 'Fish Fest.'"

The artist who'd loaned her these photo-booth props deserved a complimentary weekend at a spa or something. Too bad she didn't have the funds in her budget. She still couldn't believe that she'd pulled in so many potential clients.

The warmth of Heath's gaze kept her irrationally distracted as she worked her way through the line. Her whole body ached at this point, but she wasn't stopping until all the people waiting had had their pictures taken, and understood the instructions to look at the digital files later and order the ones that they wanted.

At last, the line dwindled to zero. With her camera strap secured around her neck and fatigue weighing her steps, she scooted behind the table and sagged onto the metal folding chair. Scout barked and scrambled around Heath to get to Lexi.

"Hi, puppers." She leaned over and gave the dog a generous scratch under the chin. "You're the main attraction here today."

Heath feigned an exasperated groan. "Don't tell him that. It'll just go to his head. Then he'll hog the sofa later when I want to watch TV."

She gave him a playful smile. "Heath Donovan, did you just make a joke?"

His mouth twitched. "Don't get used to it. I'm probably dehydrated. Here. I brought you some water."

"Thank you." She took the bottle he offered, unscrewed the cap and took a long sip.

"Do you need anything else? A snack? Decaf coffee?"

She swallowed the water and put the cap back on. "No, I brought something to eat. I need to drink water and stay off my feet. At least for a few minutes. Have you checked out the rest of the festival?"

Craning her neck, she admired the two women sitting a few tables away with gorgeous quilts on racks behind them. She'd love to stop by their booth and say hello.

"I looked around some, but Scout gets too hyper," Heath said. "This must be overstimulating."

A kid darted by clutching a helium balloon and Scout barked, then lunged.

"If you don't mind, we'll sit here a few more minutes," he said.

"Sit here for as long as you'd like." Lexi pulled a banana and a protein bar from her bag. "Can I offer you a protein bar?"

"No way." Heath frowned. "I'm not taking food from a pregnant lady."

"You're a smart man." She ripped the wrapper open. "I'm starving."

He pushed to his feet. "Let me get you something more. Do you want a hamburger?"

"No, please sit down. I'll be okay."

He slowly reclaimed his chair. He was so kind, so attentive. "You know, I wouldn't have been able to pull any of this off without you."

Heath looked away. "Don't be silly. You would've figured something out."

"Nothing like this. People are loving the photo-booth concept."

"I'm glad." His genuine smile made her pulse speed up. "You're a talented photographer, Lexi. The people of Hearts Bay need to know that."

"Thank you. I hope they'll book a holiday mini session in the fall."

"You don't need to worry about that. Everyone looked like they were having a great time." His gaze held hers and her cheeks flushed. Then she forced herself to look away. His compliment made her feel like she was walking on sunshine. The awkwardness after their kiss had faded some. They were friends. That was all they could be. It wasn't right, making him think she wanted more.

What was he thinking, joining Lexi and her family for dinner?

Heath sat at the far end of a long table at The Tide Pool, wishing he'd opted for a quiet meal at home in front of the TV. Instead, he'd allowed Lexi and her sister Rylee to persuade him that he didn't need to spend another Saturday night alone.

Okay, so that was not exactly what they'd said. But Rylee had most definitely implied it. He'd even tried using his dog as an excuse. Lexi had called him out. She'd promptly suggested he take Scout home. That the poor guy was all tuckered out from an afternoon charming children and grown-ups at Fish Fest. She'd promised to save him a seat. They'd have to wait for a table for a large group anyway.

He grabbed his fork and stabbed another bite of salad with enough force to draw a curious glance from Asher, seated across from him. He chewed slowly, trying his best not to steal glances at Lexi. She sat to his right. Her face was animated and her hands were in constant motion as she entertained Rylee with a play-by-play of the marriage proposal she'd captured with her camera.

A part of him was glad he could spend another hour or two in Lexi's presence. But that selfish line of thinking had brought him to the very place he'd intended to avoid. Wanting what he couldn't have—a life partner, children, all the components of a happily-ever-after—was agony. Because the more time he spent with Lexi and this incredible family that she'd discovered in Hearts Bay, the bigger that icy ball of regret grew in his gut. Impossible to ignore.

"So. Heath, tell us about yourself." Mia, seated to his left, offered him a polite smile. "Lexi mentioned you're a law enforcement officer."

He wiped salad dressing from the corner of his mouth with a napkin. "That's right. I moved here from Spokane, Washington, and started in June with the police department."

"Then you must know my ex-wife, Liesel." Gus, a broad-shouldered, imposing man with brilliant blue eyes, sat on the other side of Mia.

"Yeah, we've met," Heath said. "Sometimes our shifts overlap. She's a hard worker."

"That she is." Gus reached for his soda and draped his other arm around Mia's shoulders. "How do you like Hearts Bay so far?"

Lexi's now-familiar laugh bubbled up. Heath cut a glance her way. Rylee must've said something amusing, because Lexi's eyes sparkled and her cheeks bloomed with an appealing shade of pink. His chest tightened.

Man, he was in trouble.

Heath forced himself to meet the man's gaze again and chose a benign response. "It's great so far."

Thankfully the server arrived and Mia and Gus made space for the large pizza in the middle of the table.

Lucy screeched, then flung her sippy cup on the floor, saving Heath from sharing any more of his thoughts about Hearts Bay. Gus had an intimidating presence. Even though Heath barely knew the guy, he feared somehow Gus sensed Heath's attraction toward Lexi. That wasn't something he wanted to become public information.

Cameron heaved a dramatic sigh. "Lucy. Come *on*."

Laughter rippled through the group at the table.

The boy slid from his chair, retrieved the cup from under the table and set it in front of his dad's place.

Lucy's face crumpled and she burst into tears. Her pathetic wail drew plenty of looks from other customers sitting in booths nearby. The server returned with a second pizza. Heath's stomach growled as he eyed the ham-and-pineapple-with-extra-cheese concoction the server set between him and Lexi.

The woman pulled a stack of extra napkins from her apron and placed them on the table. "Enjoy."

"Thank you for sharing a pizza with me." Lexi smiled

at Heath. "No one else in this family seems to share my affection for ham and pineapple."

"No problem." He stopped short of confessing he would've eaten just about any topping on his pizza to make her happy. How pathetic.

Activity in the crowded restaurant and Lucy's crying stilted the conversation at their end of the table. Asher placated his daughter with a small bowl of plain pasta noodles.

"Lexi, are you looking forward to the toddler years yet?" Mia teased.

Heath lifted a slice of pizza from the platter and added it to Lexi's plate.

Her eyes grew wide. "The toddler years? I can't even think about those. I'm just trying to get mentally prepared for labor and delivery."

Heath plated a slice of pizza for himself.

"Although, to be perfectly honest, I do hope to have more than one child someday," Lexi admitted softly.

The pizza server slipped from his hand and clattered onto the table. "Sorry." Heath hastily retrieved it, hoping no one noticed his hand trembling. She wanted more kids?

Sitting here with Lexi and her family, enjoying a meal after a busy day at the festival, could almost make a guy forget about the circumstances looming in the future. Until the beautiful woman sitting beside him had shared that particular dream. The reminder washed in like the waves crashing on the rocky beach at the edge of the island. Yet another reason why he couldn't be a part of her life. There was no way he'd pass his warped genetics on to anyone else.

"Gus, how old is your daughter?" Lexi asked.

"Poppy is three and a half." Gus shifted his gaze to Heath. "She's with Liesel this weekend."

Heath nodded and reached for his soda. Three-year-olds, babies, preteens. All a mystery to him. He was way out of his element here.

Conversation ebbed and flowed between the best supplies for caring for a new baby to the preschool options on the island. Heath grew increasingly uncomfortable. All topics he'd never have to know about. The longer he sat there, loneliness tightened its grip like a fist around his heart. Squeezing away the hope. He'd never get to be a dad. Never have to debate the pros and cons of half-day versus full-day kindergarten. Or which swing worked the best to soothe a fussy infant.

He'd never play baseball with his son or applaud a daughter's performance at a recital or concert.

The pizza, which had moments ago tasted amazing, seemed bland now. He forced down another bite and tried to morph his facial expression into something that looked like interest. Perhaps his mom and his brother had been right. Maybe he should have given moving here more careful thought. Lexi's shoulder brushed against his. The brief contact sent an electrifying sensation zipping across his chest. Straight to his heart. The feeling unnerved him. So moving to Hearts Bay hadn't been all bad. He got to be Lexi's neighbor and friend.

Unfortunately, that was all he could ever be.

Chapter Eight

"Don't look now, but there's a handsome dude headed this way." Rylee gently nudged Lexi's shoulder.

Lexi turned and surveyed the atrium of Hearts Bay Community Church. "Where?"

"No, don't let him catch you staring." Rylee tugged on Lexi's sleeve. "You're going to have to learn to be more discreet."

Lexi chuckled. "The guy in the expensive shoes? Almost every woman in this room is watching him right now. I'm hardly going to stand out from the crowd."

In his midthirties with sandy-blond hair, a fit athletic build and an easy smile, the man Rylee had pointed out worked his way among the people still mingling after church. She couldn't hear what he was saying, but his confident demeanor indicated he'd been assigned a mission of some sort. His chambray shirt paired with green corduroy trousers and clog-style leather designer shoes had already drawn a few curious stares. That wasn't exactly the standard outfit for most of the guys who lived in Hearts Bay and attended this church.

"He looks like he's trying to get people to volunteer for something," Lexi said.

"Hmm. Probably the youth group's fall retreat." Rylee tossed her dark hair over her shoulder. "It's always a struggle finding enough adults to chaperone."

Lexi turned to Annie, who was standing on the other side of Rylee. "Has he been by the coffee shop yet?"

Annie glanced up from her phone. A flush rose to her cheeks. Interesting.

"I haven't met him. His sister is married to the pastor. Their dad is the new manager at the resort." A muscle ticked under Annie's eye. "I heard he moved here from Utah or Arizona."

Lexi traded a glance with Rylee.

Rylee's brows rose in a slow arch. "When he comes over here, you can clarify."

"Nope." Annie shook her head. "Not happening."

"He's talking to Mrs. Hale now," Rylee added. "Looks like they're coming our way. I'm sure she'll introduce you."

Annie tucked her phone into her pocket. Her eyes darted between the approaching man and the nearest exit. "I'm going to head out."

"Oh, no, you don't." Rylee linked her arm through Annie's and tugged her closer. "Stay here. Let's see what he's up to."

Annie's shoulders wilted. "Rylee, now is not a good time."

"Hello, ladies." A woman dressed head to toe in black, with short spiky hair and audacious animal-print earrings swiveling from her ears, stopped in front of Lexi. She extended her hand. "I'm Sharon Hale, Asher's mother. I don't believe we've met."

"It's nice to meet you, Mrs. Hale." She shook the friendly woman's hand. "I'm Lexi Thomas."

"Ladies, I'd like you to meet my new friend, Noah Kendrick. Noah, this is Lexi Thomas, Rylee Madden and Annie Woodland."

"Ladies, it's a pleasure to meet you." Noah shook each of their hands and offered a friendly smile.

Was it her imagination or did his grasp on Annie's hand linger just a second longer?

The color on her friend's cheeks deepened two shades. Rylee's grip on Annie's arm tightened. Oh, poor woman. She looked miserable.

Noah tucked his hands in his front pants pockets. "I'm helping my sister and brother-in-law find more volunteers for the youth lock-in on Saturday night. Are any of you available to help?"

"That's not my jam." Rylee played with the long strands of her hair. "I'll pass."

Amusement sparked in Noah's green eyes. "Not my jam, either, but we're all in this together. Hearts Bay's youth group has grown, and there are more tweens and teens signed up than my sister and her husband can handle. What do you say? Why don't we all chip in and give a few hours of our time to help these wonderful kids celebrate the start of a new school year?"

"Persuasive speech, but it's still a no for me," Rylee said. "Perhaps you should consider running for the school board or mayor next?"

Noah's grin widened. "I just might do that. Thanks for the suggestion."

"I'll be glad to help." Lexi raised her hand. "How do I sign up?"

Noah retrieved his phone from his back pocket and

handed it to her. "If you add your contact info, I'll be in touch shortly. Annie, how about you?"

Annie's fingers trembled as she tucked a strand of hair behind her ear. "No, I don't think so."

Her words came out barely more than a whisper. Wow. Lexi felt for her. Her warm, extroverted friend who had customers' coffee orders memorized and ran a successful business had morphed into a nervous woman who could barely maintain eye contact.

"I could ask my next-door neighbor." Lexi handed Noah's phone to him. Oh, she regretted the words as soon as they'd left her mouth. She'd wanted to do something to help steer Noah's attention away from Annie. But volunteering Heath without his permission might be overstepping.

"Sweet." Noah took his phone. "What's his name?"

"Heath Donovan. He's a police officer and he's not usually off on Saturdays, but he might be able to help for a few hours."

"Perfect. The lock-in won't start until six, so hopefully he can come straight here after work," Noah said. "Can I have his number?"

"Let me ask him first and I'll get back to you," Lexi said.

They said goodbye and parted ways. Mrs. Hale guided Noah toward more potential volunteers chatting nearby. Heath would probably try to bail once she told him the details. Did he even go to church? Surely he cared about the youth on the island. He'd been away in Anchorage all week. Much to her disappointment, he'd insisted on sending Scout to a kennel, even though she'd offered to keep the sweet dog at her house.

To be honest, she'd missed them both. But she couldn't

exactly ask him to spend a Saturday evening alone with her. Not when she'd kissed him, then promptly declared it a mistake. Volunteering as chaperones was a perfect excuse for them to spend several hours together. Now all she had to do was convince him to sign up.

After spending a week away from Orca Island, there was one thing Heath knew for sure. He'd missed Lexi. And he desperately needed an excuse to see her.

The mandatory in-service for police officers in Anchorage had been well worth his time. He'd returned to Hearts Bay feeling better informed and more equipped to handle domestic violence scenarios as an officer on duty.

Scout pranced around the entryway, his tail swishing against Heath's legs.

"I see you, buddy."

Heath set his backpack and suitcase down, then closed the door and sank to his knees. He'd picked Scout up from the new dog kennel a little while ago. The owner said they'd had a fantastic time together. Scout had whined and panted in the back of the truck all the way home. Heath trusted the woman, but he still felt a tiny bit guilty. This dog was growing on him. He compensated by giving Scout a thorough ear scratch.

Scout leaned in and rewarded Heath with a sloppy swipe of his tongue across his cheek.

Heath chuckled. "You're a good dog. I missed you."

The Goldendoodle whined, slathered Heath's face with a parting kiss, then ran and grabbed his blue stuffed gorilla.

"Oh, I almost forgot." He unzipped his bag and

pulled out a squeaky cheeseburger-shaped toy. "Check out what I got for you."

Scout stood still, eyeing the toy, his tail wagging.

"Come on, boy." Heath went into the kitchen. Scout trailed after him. After quickly removing the tags, he tossed the toy down the hallway. The dog barked, then raced after it, his nails clattering across the hardwood floor. He jumped on the toy, plucked it off the floor and raced back to Heath.

They played several rounds of fetch. The whole time, images of Lexi spooled through his head. Her brilliant smile. The aroma of her shampoo lingering in his truck after she'd ridden in the front seat. Or the way she'd gasp in surprise, then snap a photo of something beautiful, which happened often around here. Alaska did not disappoint, especially this time of year. Leaves had turned a brilliant shade of yellow. The air carried a crisp bite. A faint powdered-sugar dusting of snow appeared on the tip of Mount Larsen.

He liked her. A lot. And he wasn't confident he could keep pretending that he didn't. His family's health history was bleak, though. That wasn't a fact he could ignore.

He played with Scout for a few more minutes, until the dog dropped the toy and nudged his empty bowls. Heath fed him and made sure he had plenty of clean, fresh water before settling on the sofa with his laptop.

He streamed a professional football game on television, mostly as background noise to overpower the sound of Scout's obnoxious eating habits. Heath had been thinking all day about doing more research on Huntington's, but that required privacy. Sleuthing on his personal device. A degenerative condition wasn't a topic he wanted to read about while sitting next to his fellow officers on the small plane flying back to Hearts Bay.

Heath opened the browser, swiped his clammy palms on his jeans, then searched for Huntington's disease and genetic testing. He'd done the search before, but somehow he'd hoped that maybe things would be different. Maybe new information would surface. A road map that would offer encouragement. Hope. He longed for a scenario where he wasn't saddled with the possibility of a shortened life span, marked by suffering and loss of cognitive function. A slow fade that left his loved ones traumatized.

He kept scrolling until he found an article from a trusted source. If he didn't show any symptoms, then he didn't really need to be tested. Some people with similar genetic history to his chose to get tested to see if they were carriers and others chose not to find out at all. He'd always happily camped in the not-knowing land. But meeting Lexi had changed everything.

Scout stood from his bed near the fireplace and ambled over. His tail wagged as he rested his chin on Heath's leg.

His chest squeezed. He ran his palm through Scout's curly hair. What a perceptive animal. "Thanks for the love, pal."

His phone pinged.

I know you're probably watching the football game tonight and I'm so sorry to bother you, but is there any way you could come over here and help me? I'm trying to put a bookshelf together for the baby's room. Bookshelf: 3 and Lexi: 0

Heath smiled at Lexi's text message, then powered off his TV without checking the score. Who cared about football? He hadn't seen her in seven days. That was about seven days too many. Scout raced to the door, barking.

"How do you know where I'm going?"

No point in trying to get his dog to stay in his crate now. Clearly he'd invited himself along. Scout tossed his head and gave Heath the side-eye. His body language telegraphed an unmistakable canine message.

Go ahead. Leave me. I dare you.

"No worries. I know better than to go over there without you." Heath clicked Scout's leash onto his collar. "Come on, buddy. We'd better grab some tools."

They went out to the garage, where Heath grabbed a small portable toolbox. Then they walked next door. Scout strained against the leash, urging Heath to close the short distance between the houses as quickly as possible.

Heath and Scout bounded up the porch steps. The canine sat down on the brown mat with the words *Happy Fall Y'all* on it and stared at the front door. Heath rang Lexi's doorbell.

"Look at you with your manners. I had no idea you were such a gentleman."

The tip of Scout's tail swished back and forth.

Heath's pulse thrummed with anticipation. Assembling furniture was probably his least favorite household task, but if that was what she needed, then that was what he'd do.

The door swung open. "Hey."

Her brilliant smile nearly took him to his knees. Scout tried to jump on her but Heath held him back.

"Hey." He managed to squeeze out that one measly syllable. Man, she was beautiful. Her abdomen was perfectly round underneath her long white T-shirt. The hem of her long gray cardigan sweater brushed against her black leggings.

He gestured toward her moccasin-style slippers. "No boot?"

"No boot." She stepped back and motioned for them to come inside. "Mia said I can go without for an hour or two a day. I'm so happy I don't have to see a surgeon off the island."

"Rock on." He held out his fist for her to bump.

Rock on? Nobody had said that since 1993. And since when did he fist-bump a lady?

She brushed her knuckles against his. Always polite, even when he made things awkward. Then Scout barked, demanding Lexi's attention. For once he was grateful he'd brought the unruly dog along. At least he'd deflect attention from his own embarrassing behavior.

"Hello, there, handsome," she crooned, leaning down and giving the dog a generous pat on the head. "Follow me. I have treats for humans and for dogs."

Scout barked again and trotted into the kitchen like he lived there.

"Oh, brother." Heath gently closed the door. "And he was behaving so well. I was super proud there for a minute."

"I hate to admit it, but he has trained me," Lexi called over her shoulder. "He gets a treat almost every time he comes over."

"Noooo," Heath groaned and tipped his head back. "You had me fooled. I thought you were teaching him only good things."

"I did teach him a few good things. Watch this." She held a closed fist over his head. "Scout, sit."

He immediately sat down in a regal poodle-like pose.

"Wow, that's impressive."

"I know, right?" She dropped the biscuit on the floor. Scout snarfed it down. "On his best days I can get him to roll over, but that one's a little hit-or-miss."

"You're miles ahead of me," Heath confessed. "I haven't taught him a single trick."

She lifted one slender shoulder. "There's still time for him to learn plenty. Come on—I'll show you this bookshelf. Also known as the bane of my existence."

Heath followed her down the hallway. She flipped on the light in the bedroom. The walls had been painted a soft yellow. Gray-and-white-striped curtains framed the window.

"This is supposed to be a bookshelf." She gestured to some boards and a plastic packet of hardware lying on the beige carpet. "I got the crib and changing table already, and the dresser is supposed to be arriving in a couple of weeks."

Heath surveyed the room. "You put those together?"

"No, team Madden to the rescue. They painted and moved the furniture in here. I wanted to at least do one thing myself." She wrinkled her nose in a way that he found so totally adorable. "But I can't get this bookshelf to cooperate."

"Let me take a look."

Scout trotted into the room with a toy in his mouth. Heath shot him a pointed look. "Not happening, dude. This isn't about you."

Lexi laughed. "Aw, Scout. I'll play with you."

She stood in the doorway, tossing the toy toward the

living room. Scout happily retrieved it. Heath set his toolbox down and perused the directions.

"So, I did a thing…" Lexi said. "Feel free to say no, but I gave your name as a potential volunteer to chaperone part of the youth lock-in at church on Saturday night."

Her words tumbled out in a rush. He methodically arranged screws and sorted washers, processing her confession. A youth lock-in? That sounded like the opposite of a good time. And church? He hadn't attended in a very long time. "Are you volunteering?"

"For a few hours. Not overnight."

Anxiety skittered across his skin. He was more nervous about the church part than the youth being trapped inside the building for their own amusement.

If he said yes, he'd get to hang out with Lexi for a few hours, though. "Sure, I'll do it."

She gasped. "Really? I'm so glad! Let me text my contact person right quick."

Her footsteps tracked down the hall toward the kitchen. Scout went with her. Heath reached for the materials he needed to assemble the bookshelf.

Helping her felt so normal. So domestic. And it scared him.

Because he wanted so much to be a part of this life that Lexi had built for herself. The baby's furniture in the room, the faint sound of her bracelets jangling together and the pleasant aroma of something sweet baking in the oven floating down the hallway all made him yearn for more.

If it weren't for Huntington's, he could be more than her neighbor and friend. He caught sight of three tiny baby outfits hanging in the closet and he had to look away. This wasn't fair.

* * *

So maybe they should have volunteered at the animal shelter instead.

Lexi winced as a red playground ball zinged by, narrowly missing Heath's head before it slammed into the wall in the church's multipurpose room.

"Oops. Sorry!" yelled a teenage boy standing about twenty feet away wearing a T-shirt and gym shorts. He swooped his unruly dark brown hair out of his eyes, then held up his palm to collect the ball.

"No problem." Heath picked up the ball and rolled it back to him.

When he straightened, she glimpsed the lines tightening around his mouth.

He looked aggravated. Regret threaded through her. "Maybe I should have thought this through before I volunteered us."

"It's all right." Heath linked his arms across his chest. "We're leaving in a few hours. How bad could it be?"

All of a sudden, a girl abandoned the dodgeball game and sprinted toward the trash can by the door. Except she didn't quite make it and lost her dinner all over the floor.

"Oh, my." Lexi's stomach heaved and she turned away. She clapped her hand over her mouth.

The place smelled like dirty socks and pizza. Not a great combination, especially when her sense of smell was particularly sensitive these days.

"Are you going to be okay?" Heath rested his hand on her shoulder. "Do you need to step outside and get some fresh air?"

She shook her head, then lowered her hand and took a cautious breath. "I'm okay."

"Hang on. I'll get you something to drink." Heath strode toward the double doors leading into the church's kitchen. Lexi leaned against the wall and tried to keep a watchful eye on the two teams of kids playing dodgeball. Thankfully someone on staff had dispatched another volunteer to clean up the mess on the floor. An older woman had gently guided the young girl out of the gym. Maybe dodgeball after dinner was a poor choice. Although she'd rather supervise this activity than the pie-eating contest or the pumpkin catapult happening outside.

Heath returned and handed her a can of lemon-lime soda. "Will this help?"

"Yes. Thank you." She took the cold aluminum can, her fingers brushing against his. Her heart responded with a not-so-subtle thrumming against her ribs. Oh, brother. Not that she was ready to deliver her baby just yet, but she would not miss these roller-coaster hormones.

She cracked the soda open and took a few small sips. The sweet, carbonated drink settled her stomach.

This had been her wild idea. A ploy because she wanted to spend time with Heath. Maybe she deserved to be nauseous for scheming like a teenage girl just to spend a few hours standing inside a church next to him.

"Did your church do any lock-ins when you were in high school?"

An expression she couldn't quite decipher flitted across Heath's face. "I stopped going to church after seventh grade. Sort of lost interest."

He didn't elaborate and she got a distinct feeling that he didn't want to.

"So, no lock-ins, then?"

He shook his head.

One of the dodgeball players landed an especially effective shot to an opponent's back, nailing the girl directly between the shoulder blades. She released a high-pitched screech, then stumbled into the arms of her nearest teammate.

Lexi grimaced. "Do you think she's injured?"

A muscle under Heath's eye twitched. They both watched carefully until the game resumed. The girl appeared to be fine. She picked up the ball and hurled it toward the boy who'd eliminated her from the game before racing out of the room, laughing.

"We always had so much fun at youth group when I was a kid," Lexi said. "I didn't appreciate what I had at the time, but now I'm grateful. Growing up in a small town seemed so boring then. However, we were truly blessed to have people who wanted to invest in us. To help us grow. How about you? What kind of things did you do to keep busy?"

"The usual kid stuff. Rode our bikes and played sports."

"Did your parents ever send you to church camp?" she asked. "I was so sad the first year they dropped me off. I didn't know a soul, and the older campers teased us about leeches in the lake. But by the end of my two weeks there, I couldn't wait to go back the next summer."

Heath didn't answer right away. Oh, there went the arms crossed against his chest again. The twitch under the eye had progressed to his jaw knotting tight. Yikes. Maybe this wasn't his scene at all. She shouldn't have volunteered him for something he really didn't want to do. Or maybe she just talked too much.

The doors opened and Noah stepped in. He scanned the room. When he spotted them, he strode their way. "Can one of you give us a hand outside, please? There's a glow-in-the-dark tag game going down that needs extra supervision."

"I'm in." Heath offered Lexi a smile that didn't quite meet his eyes. "I'll catch up with you later."

Oh. Okay, then. Feeling as deflated as a forgotten balloon after a party, she took her place leaning against the wall and slowly sipped her soda. She'd been motivated by Noah's mini speech after church last Sunday. What a nice guy, drumming up volunteers for his sister and her husband so they weren't overwhelmed in their ministry. He'd said all the right things to appeal to her own positive experiences at church youth events. Combined with Annie's obvious embarrassment about seeing Noah and Rylee's snarky response to his request, she'd felt compelled to step up. Hearts Bay had been so welcoming and encouraging to her. She would've really been in a pickle if not for the kindness of folks in this community.

But she'd obviously provoked Heath. Had he had a bad experience at church? Come to think of it, she didn't know anything about his family or his past. Since he was a police officer, she'd assumed he was an upstanding guy. And he had to have cleared a background check to even be here tonight.

She was probably overthinking this.

But the longer she stood there alone, chaperoning the activities, the more doubt crept in. She'd been foolish in using the volunteer opportunity as an excuse to spend more time with him. What a mistake. He obviously did not want anything to do with this church. Or maybe he just didn't want anything to do with her.

He hadn't meant to be rude. Really, he hadn't.

But Lexi had started asking him questions about his family life and poking around his reasons for not attending youth group back home in Spokane. He'd panicked. The words wouldn't flow.

When Noah had shown up and offered him a lifeline to leave the dodgeball game, like a coward, he'd slipped out the door. Being outside in the damp cold air, supervising a group of rowdy teenagers running around in the dark, had been a lot less fun than the dodgeball thing. But at least outside he'd been able to isolate himself and focus on the task at hand without anyone asking him too many questions about his past or his church experience.

And that was the way he wanted it.

At least that was what he kept telling himself. He slid more weights on either end of the bar, then reclined on the padded bench in the police station's weight room. Gripping the bar with both hands, he pushed up, starting another set of fifteen repetitions. Sweat soaked his T-shirt, and he strained under the burden of the added weight. The incline bench press had always been his nemesis. He'd never been able to lift more than 120 pounds consistently. And certainly not for more than ten repetitions. But today he was determined. If for no other reason than to prove to himself that he could.

"Need a spotter, bro?" Kevin called from across the room, where he'd finished probably his eighth set of a gazillion repetitions on the lat pull-down machine. The guy aggravated him, but Heath had to give him credit. Kevin was the most physically fit guy on the force.

"Nope." Heath grunted. "I'm...good."

So that wasn't exactly true, either. He could push through the physical pain and finish this set, but there wasn't a quick resolution to his emotional distress. Guilt had crept in the second he'd seen the hurt in Lexi's eyes. He still felt bad for walking away so abruptly. The alternative meant telling her everything. How a cloud of grief and loss loomed over his teenage years because of his father's declining health. Then he'd have to explain the real reason that he didn't want to go to church—he was still angry at the Lord. The grand finale of his confession would focus on the scourge of Huntington's disease wrapping its vicious tentacles around the branches of his family tree. It was all too much. He wouldn't be a burden to her. Because after he'd witnessed his father's horrific decline drain his mother's physical, mental and emotional energy, he vowed he'd never put someone he loved in that position.

His attraction toward Lexi wasn't going away, though. He didn't want to avoid her. That would only make him more miserable. Scout spent two days at her house and three at the dog day care. The number of pens, pairs of shoes and kitchen spatulas the animal had destroyed since Heath had adjusted his routine indicated Scout was not on board with this new plan. Spending more time at the kennel and dog day care than he did at Lexi's house likely would provoke more misbehavior.

How had it come to this? Scout *owned* him. All because of his attraction toward the woman who lived next door.

Heath's muscles screamed for relief, but he pushed

through the pain and finished the tenth repetition. After racking the weight, he slid out from under the bar and sat up. Classic rock music blared from somebody's portable speaker sitting on the shelf nearby. The room smelled like perspiration and the synthetic rubber mats on the floor. He grabbed his towel and mopped the sweat from his face.

"Nice work, my man." Kevin strode over and clapped him on the shoulder. "Want me to spot you on the next set?"

Heath shook his head.

"All right, just thought I'd ask." Kevin grinned. "A few of us are headed over to Maverick's to hang. Want to join us?"

"No, thanks." Heath stood and swung the towel over his shoulder. "Gotta get my dog from day care."

"Right." Kevin nodded. "See you around."

Heath retrieved his water bottle from the floor and drained its contents. He'd done the work. Pushed his body to its limits. But the satisfaction was short-lived.

He still felt like a wounded animal hemmed in on all sides by a vicious predator. Living a solitary life grew less and less appealing with each passing day. Not that he wanted to leave Hearts Bay. So far he'd had a great experience living here. Island life wasn't as treacherous as he'd once imagined. But since he'd met Lexi and her family and experienced a small taste of what it was like to spend time with her, he really didn't want to keep pushing her away.

Except what choice did he have? She had already said that she wanted to have more children someday. Maybe she would change her mind after she had one, but what if she didn't? She was kind, beautiful and fearless. Standing in the way of her hopes and dreams wasn't right. If he wanted to be a part of her future, he'd have to be honest about Huntington's.

He just couldn't bring himself to go there. Not yet. Maybe not ever.

Chapter Nine

Two agonizing weeks later, Rylee drove Lexi to Hearts Bay's community center, insisting that she had a surprise waiting. Lexi's fall photo shoot had been scheduled for several weeks. She'd already asked to use a small section of the lawn outside the building to take her clients' photos. Thankfully the parks and recreation director had said yes.

Rylee pulled into the parking lot outside the community center. "Here. Put this on."

Lexi eyed the pink sleep mask in Rylee's hand. "Seriously?"

She wasn't in the mood for any surprises.

"Come on—please? I promise this will be fun. You're going to love everything about this."

Lexi heaved a dramatic sigh. "Fiiiiine."

She snatched the mask and put the dumb thing on. Obviously Rylee wanted nothing to do with her protests.

Twelve families had booked appointments. Initially, Lexi had hoped for fifteen or maybe even eighteen. But at this point in her pregnancy she was grateful for the more manageable number. Meeting with eighteen different families would've been more than her aching hips and poor lower back could handle in one day.

She slowly climbed out of the car and stood, blindfolded. The morning sunshine offered little warmth. Lexi shivered in the crisp fall air.

"We're almost there. Keep your eyes closed." Rylee gently guided Lexi by the shoulders away from the vehicle. Now that they were out of the car and moving in a mysterious direction, she deeply regretted giving in to her sister's antics. Her choice of footwear was a mistake, too. The fracture had healed, but she still wasn't supercomfortable in anything other than slippers or sneakers.

"I'm an awkward, clumsy pregnant lady trying to walk on grass in boots. Do you think that's a good idea to keep me blindfolded?"

"Good point." Riley squeezed her shoulders again and brought her to a stop. "Okay, we're here. Take the blindfold off."

Finally. Lexi lifted the mask from her head.

"Surprise!" Mackenzie, Tess, Mia and Annie flung their arms wide, hands shimmying. They stood on the lawn beside a trio of Christmas trees decorated with tasteful gold garland, white and gold ornaments and white twinkle lights. Stacks of wrapped presents in white-and-gold-striped and polka-dot paper with audacious bows flanked both sides of the trees.

A table decorated with a festive patterned tablecloth and a miniature Christmas tree centerpiece displayed portable containers of coffee and all the goodies for a hot cocoa bar.

Lexi blinked back tears. She pressed her fingertips

to her cheeks and turned in a slow circle. "Y'all. How did you...? When did you...?"

Stunned by their kindness, she couldn't even form a complete sentence.

"We got up super early and worked very hard." Rylee looped her arm around Lexi's waist and pulled her in for a quick side hug. "Also, Mom and Dad's guest cottage makes for an awesome top secret place to stash stuff we didn't want you to know about."

Annie stepped forward. "We're so happy that you're here and proud of you for growing your photography business. People are coming to get their pictures taken and we thought having snacks and treats afterward might encourage more smiles. Hope that's okay with you."

"It's more than okay." Lexi folded Annie into a hug. "This is amazing. Thank you so much! What do I owe you for the coffee and cocoa...? And are those doughnuts?"

She craned her neck to see around Annie and gave the table a more thorough examination. "Annie, you didn't have to do all that."

"I know, but I wanted to help. The Maddens are dear friends of mine, which means you're dear to me, as well."

She blinked back another wave of tears. Her chin wobbled. "Thank you. That means a lot."

"I'm happy to do it." Annie grinned and squeezed Lexi's arm. "Now, go take some amazing photos."

"And be sure and thank Heath next time you see him." Rylee tucked the pink sleep mask into her coat pocket. "He couldn't be here today, but he did a lot of the heavy lifting on this one."

"Oh, Heath." Lexi couldn't stop a smile.

Rylee gave her a knowing look.

"What?" Lexi shrugged one shoulder. "He's been a very kind friend to me. The nicest neighbor a girl could have."

"A nice neighbor. Right." Rylee winked and Lexi turned away, determined to focus on setting her camera and tripod up properly.

To be honest, she'd missed Heath. They hadn't seen much of each other lately. He'd kept his word and arranged for Scout to go to a dog day care three days a week. But Lexi had convinced him to let her keep Scout the other two days when Heath worked. When he came by to pick up Scout at the end of the day, they exchanged polite conversation. But ever since that awkward moment at the lock-in, he'd kept her at arm's length.

She'd tried not to take it personally. And she wasn't about to ask him what had happened. Her heart couldn't take his honest response. Besides, there were plenty of items on her to-do list demanding attention. The first half of September had been a blur of getting ready for the baby, taking a birthing class and meeting with Mackenzie whenever they could squeeze it in to figure out how she could launch an online course about photography. She hadn't really had time to focus on anything else and tried not to dwell on the fact that she'd once daydreamed about a relationship with Heath.

It wasn't meant to be.

Dr. Rasmussen had said she and her baby were in great health and he didn't have any concerns. She still couldn't quite wrap her mind around the fact that she was going to be someone's mother. In less than three months she would be solely responsible for the care of a brand-new, completely helpless human.

"Lexi, where would you like us to put a table to check people in?" Mackenzie's question pulled her back to reality.

Come on. Stay focused.

Everything she had done so far since August had set her up for today's event. She had clients who'd be here anytime now to get their pictures taken. And she needed to be ready. Her friends had worked hard and rallied around her so that she could make this vision for her small business happen. Now was not the time to get bogged down in what might have been. There wasn't room in her life for a romantic relationship. It wasn't fair to her or her baby.

If she didn't give her clients today her full attention, that wasn't fair, either. Sure, these were just family portrait sessions, not rocket science or brain surgery. But these photos offered priceless memories, and she'd promised to make today's holiday mini sessions happen.

"Here you go." Mia set Lexi's camera bag and tripod on the ground. "I brought what was in the back of Rylee's car. Did we miss anything?"

"Nope, this is perfect. Thank you." She unpacked her camera equipment and got to work setting up. Providing excellent service meant she'd be able to sell more photo packages, hopefully earn more money and solidify her reputation in the community as a wonderful photographer. Those had been her goals all along. She couldn't let her erratic emotions and thoughts of a certain handsome police officer distract her.

* * *

"Scout, let's go." Heath stood by the front door and jangled his car keys.

The ornery dog sat on his bed, his stuffed blue gorilla wedged under his chin. He pinned Heath with a disgusted look.

"Don't you want to go for a ride?" He forced enthusiasm into his voice. Scout heaved a deep sigh.

Oh, brother. "What's with all the drama? I thought you loved riding in the car?"

Scout blinked at him, as if he couldn't be bothered. Heath didn't have any issue letting him stay in his crate while he ran errands. But the dog seemed to enjoy being included. Going places. Interacting with humans. Wasn't that why he always wanted to go next door and visit Lexi?

"Am I really going to have to bribe you? All right. Fine." Heath reached for the doorknob. "What if I promise you a treat?"

Scout's ears lifted. He still didn't get up, though.

"Will that motivate you to get in the car? I'll tell you what. If you'll ride to the hardware store with me, we'll stop and see Annie for a cup of homemade whipped cream."

Scout leaped from his bed and raced toward the door.

"You're a goofy dog, you know that?" He opened the door just in time for Scout to skid through the gap. The animal didn't even bother with the steps. Just skipped them completely and went straight to the driveway. Then he raced around the yard in tight circles, his pink tongue spilling from his open mouth.

Heath stood on the porch, watching in disbelief.

A few minutes later, Scout slowed down. Panting,

he trotted over to a puddle in the street's gutter and slurped up water.

"Okay, that's enough." Heath opened the truck's door and motioned for Scout to climb in. On his way out of the neighborhood, Heath's thoughts turned to Lexi. *Again.* How was she spending her day? Making plans with her sisters? Getting ready for the baby's arrival?

He'd been tempted this week to stop by and tell her more about his family. Especially since his mom had called and shared about the recent development with Reid. His brother had a noticeable tremor in one of his forearm muscles. Still refused to see a doctor, of course, but the new symptom had Mom more concerned than usual.

He slowed to a stop at the end of the street. Much like the last time they'd chatted, his mother clung to her steadfast faith that God heard their prayers and would use even this for their good eventually.

How could she be so brave knowing that Reid would likely endure unspeakable suffering?

Scout whined and paced the confined area behind the driver's seat. Heath checked both ways, tapped his signal, then turned onto the street. As he drove toward the middle of Hearts Bay and the Main Street shops, Scout alternated between sitting down and immediately standing up again.

Heath shot him a look over his shoulder. "Scout, what's the matter? Need some fresh air?"

Scout stopped behind Heath, his breath warm on Heath's neck. Heath nudged the buttons in the door panel to lower the windows. Scout promptly stuck his nose to the opening and sniffed the air.

As Heath drove closer to Main Street, he signaled

to turn right and head for the hardware store. The dog started barking incessantly.

"Ow." Heath clapped one hand over his ear. "Thanks, I didn't need my hearing on that side anyway. What is going on with you?"

He slowed to a stop and checked both ways. Scout barked louder and flung his body from side to side with enough force to rock the truck.

"This is bonkers." He shifted in his seat, determined to get his hyper dog under control. "You've got to calm down."

Scout paid him no mind. Just kept pinging back and forth from one side of the cab to the other.

Heath sighed and faced forward again. He spotted the sign for The Trading Post. "Oh, I get it. You think we should go there first."

He hesitated. Was Scout really that smart? Or had he been by to see Annie so many times that he'd memorized the route? And why was Heath letting a Goldendoodle with big opinions influence his plans?

Then again, if he insisted on being in charge and went to the hardware store first, he'd pay dearly later. Whatever he purchased would likely get chewed up. Even if he was extra careful and stowed the painting supplies on a high shelf in the garage, Scout would find some other way to express his frustration. Heath had lost a year's supply of writing utensils and crew socks already.

"Okay, you win." He lifted his hands off the steering wheel while they were still at the stop sign. "The hardware store can wait."

He changed course and turned left, angling his truck toward the coffee shop.

Scout stopped jumping around long enough to reward Heath with a generous lick on the side of his face.

"Ew." He shivered and hunched over the steering wheel. "I was not expecting that. Maybe we could work on a different method for you to express your gratitude?"

The scent of Scout's not-so-great breath permeated the truck's cab. Heath lowered the windows a smidgen more. "We'll add canine breath freshener to our next pet-store shopping list, too."

Scout barked.

Heath chuckled. "You're too smart, you know that? Too smart for your own good."

"Oh, Lexi, this is fantastic." Mackenzie clapped her hands together. "I'm so proud of you."

They sat side by side at a table in The Trading Post with Lexi's laptop open between them. "You don't think my slides are lame?"

"Of course not." Mackenzie pressed her manicured hand to Lexi's forearm. "This is an excellent presentation. Are you sure you've never done this before?"

"Not anything this elaborate." Lexi twisted her disposable coffee cup in a slow circle. "I did slide decks for a presentation in college, but never paired with an audio recording."

"No one will ever know you're a rookie digital-course instructor." Mackenzie grinned. "You've gone above and beyond. This is a ton of useful info. Your students will be thrilled."

Lexi twisted a lock of her hair around her finger. "Thank you. I'm still super nervous. The technology for instructing people on the internet feels intimidating."

She stifled a groan. Could she sound any more pathetic? This was supposed to be fun. Not to mention her best long-term strategy for making money. Maybe even passive income once she got everything up and running.

"If you want to practice on me, just let me know." Mackenzie's phone buzzed against the table. "Except not right now. I've got to go in a few minutes. My daughter's going to a sleepover tonight, and I promised my son we'd grab a pizza, then watch a movie together. My husband's on duty at the station."

"Oh, I'm sorry to keep you." Lexi closed out of the slide deck. "Thanks for meeting with me."

"You're not keeping me. I wanted to help you with this." Mackenzie slipped her phone into her handbag. "Have you thought about how much you're going to charge for the course?"

Lexi lifted one shoulder in a noncommittal shrug. "Probably not much, since it's my first one. How does fifty bucks sound?"

"*What?* No way." Mackenzie splayed her hand against her beige-and-cream-striped sweater. "You need to charge at least a hundred."

Lexi coughed, nearly spraying decaf mocha all over her computer. "One hundred dollars? For an online course about how to take better pictures of your kids?"

"Yes, girl." Mackenzie pinned her with a long look. "You would be shocked to know what people charge for classes that are similar to yours, but don't provide nearly as much value."

Lexi stopped short of asking the woman how many

online courses she'd taken to have developed so much knowledge. Maybe she didn't want to know the answer to that. She dabbed at her mouth with her napkin. "I'll think about it."

"Remember, this is costing you time and you are a professional." Mackenzie stood and slung her bag over her shoulder. "I still can't get over those pictures you took of our family at Fish Fest. Those are amazing."

"Oh, stop." Lexi dismissed her with a wave. "It was my pleasure."

"Let's talk soon." Her friend waggled her fingers, then headed for the exit. As she stepped outside, Heath and Scout came in.

Lexi's eyes locked with Heath's and her breath caught. Scout trotted over to the table and rubbed against her leg.

"Hi, there, boy." She pushed back her chair and trailed her fingers along his spine. "What are you doing here?"

Heath caught up and grabbed Scout's collar. "You shouldn't be in here without a leash."

Lexi glanced around the coffee shop. "They aren't that busy. I don't think Annie minds."

"I mind," Heath said. "Animals aren't supposed to be off leash in public places."

Ah, yes. Even an off-duty police officer probably couldn't stand to ignore the statutes or laws or whatever they were called. She started to mention that Annie didn't seem to enforce that rule, then thought better of it.

"I promised him some whipped cream, so I'd better follow through on that."

"Scout can sit here with me while you order." Lexi patted the side of her leg. "Sit down, Scout."

The dog dutifully sat beside her and proudly tossed his head.

Heath frowned. "Thanks. I'll be right back."

Lexi kept one hand on Scout's head and used her other to shut down her computer. She wasn't trying to hide her plans to teach a digital course. But her conversation with Mackenzie about price points had left her feeling more uncertain than when she'd sat down. The confidence she'd gained in her abilities after Fish Fest and the fall photo shoot had already evaporated. Being a photographer wasn't something she wanted to discuss with Heath right now.

She sneaked a glance as he stood at the counter and placed his order with the barista. A nervous feeling slithered through her insides. After her photo shoot had ended, she'd texted Heath and thanked him for helping her sisters set up everything. He'd responded with a polite but brief message. Their handoffs with the dog had been uneventful. However, she still sensed there was something he wasn't telling her. Something he was holding back. Or maybe she had an overactive imagination. Besides, he wasn't obligated to tell her anything.

Chapter Ten

Heath unfolded the plastic drop cloth and spread it over the beige carpet, then maneuvered the metal ladder into place. Mom and Reid had bought their plane tickets. They were scheduled to arrive in Hearts Bay three days before Christmas and planned to stay through New Year's Day. So he had two months to prepare both of his extra bedrooms for their visit. A twin bed, a basic nightstand and a dresser that had belonged to his grandparents filled the smallest bedroom across the hall. Reid would be fine staying in there.

Stripping the hideous wallpaper in this larger bedroom had taken much longer than he'd expected. The contractor who'd installed the fence had recommended someone to finish the task and repair the damaged drywall. Heath had gladly hired the guy. But he'd decided to handle the painting.

Mostly because he needed a distraction while Lexi was away.

Scout heaved a deep sigh and sank to the ground in the hallway outside the bedroom.

"Sorry, buddy. No dogs allowed." He'd blocked the

bedroom doorway with dining room chairs to keep Scout away from the paint. The ornery fella had spent the last ten minutes pacing the hallway, whining, then stood on the other side of the chairs, panting and giving Heath his most dejected look.

Heath avoided eye contact and unwrapped the new packages of paintbrushes and rollers. Then he turned on the extra lamps he'd brought in from the living room and master bedroom. The sun set early this time of year. He couldn't rely on the fading afternoon light from outside to illuminate the room enough for him to paint well.

Lexi was supposed to be flying back to the island today. The weather had been a little bit iffy. Hopefully her trip back from Anchorage was uneventful. He'd spent way too much time today worrying about her. Dr. Rasmussen had given his blessing for her to travel, even though she was seven weeks from her due date. Mia had concurred it was okay for her to fly, but Lexi's decision to spend a girls' weekend away made him nervous.

Not that he had any right to question her choices. Especially when her doctor and Mia both gave her the green light to travel. But he'd feel better knowing that she was home safe next door instead of hurtling across the ocean in a metal tube.

She'd been friendly whenever their paths crossed. Their conversation at the coffee shop had been polite. Enjoyable even. Although far too short for his liking. And she'd baked a batch of scrumptious cookies after he'd assembled her nursery furniture. Scout seemed to live for the two days a week he spent with Lexi. On the days when Heath picked him up from his other dog day care, they'd get home and Scout would chew up something forbidden or knock over his water bowl as soon as Heath filled it. What a feisty animal.

Heath popped the lid off the paint can, then poured the grayish-beige paint into the metal tray. He'd spent a few hours yesterday taping off all the white trim. It had been a long time since he'd painted a whole room alone, but he needed a project.

Scout heaved a pathetic sigh and sank to the carpet. He buried his snout in his paws, the hair above his eyes twitching as his chocolaty-brown gaze tracked Heath's every move.

"Don't even try that look with me." Heath selected a paintbrush from his new collection, then picked up the tray and carefully climbed the ladder. Balancing the tray on the platform at the top of the ladder, he dipped the paintbrush into the paint and began the arduous task of cutting in around where the trim met the ceiling.

His mind drifted to his plans for the holidays. Inviting his mom and Reid to visit for Christmas felt like a risky move. Their conversations had been tense lately. A bit awkward, really. Reid hadn't been able to find another job. He still refused to go to the doctor. Heath suspected their mom was helping his brother too much. Giving him the financial and emotional support she believed he needed.

Heath wasn't thrilled about the way she was handling things, but he couldn't intervene. He added more paint on his brush, then pressed it against the drywall, using slow, careful strokes. So satisfying, transforming the room into a more modern space. Painting gave him a small sense of control when the rest of his life circumstances felt uncomfortably unknown. Helping

Lexi assemble the bookshelf for her baby's room had sparked a surprising interest in updating his own place. He wanted his house to feel less like a bachelor pad and more like a home, where his small family of three would want to celebrate the holidays. Together.

Christmas had never held the same joy that it seemed to offer other families. He'd always blamed that on his father's death, but that felt more and more like a crutch with each passing year. His lousy attitude toward Christmas and the birth of Jesus was his own responsibility. He couldn't keep blaming God for Dad's excruciating illness.

Except it was easier that way.

Heath paused, the brush suspended in the air halfway between the tray and the wall. He hadn't forgotten his promise to his mother to pray more frequently. But he also hadn't followed through. Prayer felt strange. One-sided. He was afraid to ask God for anything meaningful because the Lord hadn't answered his prayers when he'd asked Him to heal his father. Just how many times was a person supposed to keep asking when it seemed there was never a response?

Sighing, he shifted his weight, already feeling the dull ache in his neck and shoulder muscles from working on home-improvement projects all day. A short break wouldn't hurt. Scout probably needed to go outside for a few minutes anyway. He balanced his paintbrush on the edge of the tray, then took a step down on the ladder. His foot slipped. As he tried to regain his balance, he knocked over the tray. It clattered to the floor. Scout barked. The last thing he remembered before his head smacked the ladder and he fell to the ground was paint splattering on the wall and the drop cloth. Then everything went black.

Lexi settled in the middle row of Gus and Mia's SUV, then tugged the door closed. Gus had the engine running and warm air from the vents enveloped her. He turned on his headlights, illuminating the heavy wet snow falling. She still couldn't get over how quickly the weather had turned. When they'd left Anchorage, the sun had been shining. Not long after they'd taken off and turned south toward Orca Island, the pilot had warned them to expect turbulence. Their one-hour flight had been quite bumpy as he'd maneuvered the small plane through the storm.

Rylee, an experienced pilot, had reassured her that they were safe. Lexi trusted her, but she'd still white-knuckled her seat's armrests for most of the trip. She was grateful to be safely on the ground and couldn't wait to get home, fix a quick dinner, then draw a hot bath and relax.

"Aunt Wexi!" Poppy sat beside her in her car seat, clutching a baby doll. "Wook."

Lexi smiled. So cute how Poppy mispronounced some of her *l*'s. And called her *aunt*. They weren't re-lated, but Mia and Gus had introduced her as an aunt and it had stuck. Lexi reached over and playfully jig-gled the little girl's snow boot. "What's your baby's name?"

"Bibby."

"That's a beautiful name." Lexi stifled a yawn. She was exhausted from the top of her head to the tips of her toes. Her girls' weekend in Anchorage with her mother, Mia, Tess and Rylee had been more fun than she could've possibly imagined. But now she envisioned sleeping for about fourteen hours straight.

Gus twisted in the driver's seat to retrieve his seat belt. "Did you have a good time?"

"So much fun." Lexi set her purse by her feet and buckled her seat belt. "We stayed up late last night, talking for hours."

"You and Rylee talked for hours. I ran out of steam before eleven," Mia said.

Gus reached for Mia's hand. "Poppy and I missed you."

The light from the dashboard illuminated Mia's face in a silvery glow. She leaned across the console and kissed him. "I missed you both, too. So nice to be home."

Lexi's heart pinched. They were so in love.

"Daddy, you kissed!" Poppy's bubbly laugh filled the car.

Mia shifted back into her own seat, but Gus kept holding her hand. They exchanged a tender smile.

Lexi looked away and shifted her attention back to Poppy. "What have you and Bibby been doing?"

Gus and Poppy had met their flight at the tiny airport. Poppy had made Mia a picture from construction paper and handed her three pieces of chocolate. So precious. It would've been nice to have someone welcome her back to Hearts Bay. An image of Heath waiting near baggage claim with a bouquet of flowers flitted through her head.

She squelched that foolish thought right away. Heath was her friend and neighbor. Sure, their one and only kiss had been incredible, but they'd both agreed it couldn't happen again.

"I wish that Eliana could come," Lexi said. "Do you think she'll visit for the holidays?"

"She's talking about it," Mia said. "They have a busy life. It's hard for them to get back to Alaska, especially with the twins and their new little one."

Gus adjusted the windshield wipers, shifted into Drive and drove toward the airport parking lot exit. Even though Lexi had spent her whole life without knowing Mia or her biological sisters, Eliana, Tess and Rylee, she already felt incredibly close to all of them. Her biological mother and father, as well. The Maddens had welcomed her into their family without any hesitation.

Which was a stark difference from the family that raised her. They had refused to speak to Mia, their biological daughter, and had shunned Lexi ever since she'd moved to Hearts Bay. Every fall her mother, the one who'd raised her, had taken her shopping in Atlanta or sometimes Birmingham. Lexi's aunts would come along, and a few times they'd even treat themselves to a fall beach trip in Destin, Florida.

A pang of regret arced through her at the bittersweet memories. Would they ever invite her again? She loved her family back in Georgia. The pain of their rejection still stung. She'd never meant to hurt them. Discovering the Maddens had not been intentional. But once she'd known about her biological family and identified the unbelievable mix-up that had sent her and Mia home with the wrong families, she couldn't pretend that they didn't exist.

Or that the mix-up hadn't happened.

Now that she was going to become a mother herself, the threads that bound her to the people who had shaped her felt more significant than ever before. Losing Beau had taught her that life was precious. Relationships mattered.

Lord, please help us find a way to reconnect.

It was a simple prayer and this wasn't the first time she'd expressed those words. But the longing to have a connection to the people she'd always known as her parents wasn't fading. No matter how many miles separated them.

She gave herself a mental shake. No sense ruining a perfectly wonderful weekend thinking about a problem she couldn't resolve. "It would really be special if we could all be together at some point."

Mia smiled at her over her shoulder. "Mom and Dad would be thrilled."

The trip from the airport to her house passed quickly. Poppy kept them entertained with her questions and nonsensical chatter.

When Gus pulled into her driveway and parked, Lexi couldn't resist glancing toward Heath's house. There weren't any lights on. Not even a blue glow from the television. Huh. Maybe he wasn't home tonight. Not that he owed her an explanation for how he spent his free time.

"Thanks for a wonderful weekend, Mia. See you later, Poppy. 'Bye, Bibby." Lexi waved, grabbed her purse and climbed out of the car.

"You're welcome, Lexi. We'll see you soon," Mia said, waving back.

Gus retrieved her suitcase from the back of the car and set it on the driveway. Snow fell harder, coating her yard, the asphalt and her neighbors' roofs in a fresh layer of white. She still couldn't get over the amazing sound of snowflakes hitting the fabric of her jacket. It was like a thousand little whisper kisses.

"Thanks for the ride, Gus." She paused, one hand resting on the handle of her wheeled suitcase.

He slammed his vehicle's hatch closed. "Everything okay?"

She angled her head toward Heath's place. "Do you hear that?"

Gus looked over his shoulder toward Heath's house. "I don't hear anything unusual."

"That's a lot of barking." Loud, almost frantic, repetitive barking filtered through the night air. "I think something's wrong."

"Want me to knock and see if Heath answers?"

"Go ahead." Lexi towed her suitcase toward her front door and fumbled in her purse for her keys. "I have an extra key to his place. I'll grab it in case he doesn't answer and meet you there."

Mia opened the passenger door and climbed out. "What's wrong?"

"Gus will fill you in. I'll meet y'all next door." Her fingers trembled as she unlocked her front door, dragged her suitcase inside and raced to the kitchen, where she kept Heath's spare key in a drawer.

Outside, she cut a path across the lawn. Snow crunched under the soles of her new winter boots.

Gus stood on Heath's front porch. The pungent smell of car exhaust filled the air. Mia had gotten back in the vehicle and kept the engine running. Probably trying to keep Poppy distracted.

"He's not answering," Gus said. "I rang the bell twice."

Scout's barks grew louder. His claws scratched on

the other side of the door. "Oh, that poor dog." She squared her shoulders. "That's it… I'm going in." Lexi shoved the key in the lock and turned it. The dead bolt gave way and she pushed open the door. "Heath?"

A muffled grunt came from the vicinity of the sofa. Scout jumped all over her, pressing his paws to her torso. He tried to lick her face.

"It's okay, Scout. I'm here." She gently guided the dog to the floor, forcing a sense of calm into her voice that she definitely did not feel. Moving closer to the sofa, she stopped at the sight of Heath, flat on his back, a bag of frozen vegetables covering his eye and forehead. "Oh, no! What happened?"

"It's not a big deal," Heath growled, eyeing Lexi and Gus as they burst through the door. He didn't know how long he'd been lying on the sofa with a frozen bag of vegetables pressed to his head.

"We heard Scout barking, so we came to check on you." Lexi hurried toward him.

"Yeah, dude. We were worried," Gus added. "Mia's in the car. Want me to have her come in and check you over?"

The bag crinkled as he pulled it away. "No. I fell off the ladder in the guest room. I'll be fine."

Lexi grimaced and leaned closer. Her beautiful eyes scanned his face. "You've got quite the bruise around your right eye. And a goose egg on your forehead. Oh, and there's some blood on your cheek. Looks like—"

"Lexi." His tone was sharper than he'd intended. "Relax. I said I'll be fine."

Hurt flashed across her features. Man, he'd sounded

like a jerk. He half expected her to get up and leave. Instead, she clasped her hands in her lap.

Scout panted excessively, whining as he took another lap around the coffee table. "Shhh, Scout."

She reached out and slowed him down with a gentle pat on the top of his head. "It's okay. Help is here now. You can rest. Great job."

Scout sat beside Lexi and pressed his body against her legs. Heath couldn't deny he secretly appreciated her nearness right now, too. Even though his curt words and biting tone said the opposite.

"You don't have to do anything," Heath insisted. "I'll take it easy tonight, I promise."

Lexi shot Gus a worried look. He hovered behind the sofa, keeping a respectful distance, but his gaze narrowed at Heath's words.

"You don't look fine, my man." Gus tunneled his hands in the front pocket of his hoodie. "I'm no doctor, but I think that cut needs stitches."

Heath stifled a groan and gently inspected the wound above his eyebrow with his fingertips. Wincing at the pressure, he quickly abandoned that mission.

"Knock, knock." The front door opened and Mia stepped in. She had Poppy wedged on her hip. With two fingers tucked in the side of her mouth, the child clutched a baby doll to her chest with her other hand. Fresh snow dotted their hair and their jackets.

"Anything I can do to help?" Mia lowered the little girl to the floor. "This is Poppy, by the way."

"Hey, Poppy." Heath lowered his head back to the throw pillow he'd wedged against one end of the sofa.

Lexi shifted, her leg bumping gently against his arm. He didn't want her to leave, but he wasn't about to reveal his health history, either. Panic welled. If his head wasn't throbbing and the room didn't spin every time he tried to stand, he'd push to his feet and firmly show them all to the door.

But he couldn't ignore the fact that he needed medical attention. "I'm not going to the hospital."

Lexi carefully removed the half-thawed bag of vegetables. "No one is going to force you to do anything that you don't want to do."

"Good." He let his eyes fall closed. There. He didn't see double if he wasn't staring at her.

A trip to the ER meant filling out those dreaded health history forms, people poking and prodding him and being asked a dozen questions. No, thank you. There was no way he'd reveal his genetic backstory to a medical professional, and definitely not someone so closely connected to Lexi. He didn't want anyone to know about his family's battle against Huntington's disease. Not that his new friends wouldn't have empathy and compassion, because they were some of the nicest people he'd ever met.

But he didn't want their pity. Or their curious glances when word spread around the island.

Because word *would* spread. He'd learned that the hard way when his father was diagnosed.

If the chief found out, he'd call Heath in and question him about whether this mysterious disease would impact his performance at work. Which it would not because, so far, he didn't have any symptoms.

Although slipping and falling from a ladder concerned him.

"Sweetheart, can you get my backpack from the car? I have a few supplies in there."

Heath opened his eyes as Mia's question registered.

"Absolutely." Gus strode toward the door and stepped outside.

Poppy picked up Scout's stuffed gorilla and tossed it toward the kitchen. Scout trotted after it, then brought the toy back and dropped it at her feet. Poppy giggled, threw the stuffed animal again, and Scout gave chase.

Mia offered an encouraging smile. "Those two might keep each other occupied for a few minutes."

"Why don't I let you speak to him." Lexi stood and moved out of the way. His fingers itched to reach for her hand. What a ridiculous idea.

She stepped out of his line of sight. He already missed the comforting warmth of her presence beside him.

"Heath, can you tell me about what happened? Did you lose consciousness?" Mia knelt on the floor, her kind eyes surveying his face. Something about her calm demeanor made him want to tell her more.

"I was painting in the guest room. My mom and brother are coming for the holidays. Anyway, one minute I was up on the ladder painting, and the next thing I know, I've lost my balance. There's paint everywhere and I hit my head on the way down. Pretty sure I blacked out."

"For how long?"

He lifted one shoulder. "A few minutes maybe?"

Time felt stretchy. Like the elastic on a favorite pair of sweatpants. The last time he'd looked at the clock on his phone, it had been around three. Or was it four? His head throbbed. Then his stomach sloshed.

Mia braced to stand. "Do you need to vomit?"

"Oh, dear." Lexi's voice floated in from somewhere close by. "I'll find a bucket or something."

Heath forced himself to draw a deep breath. "I—I'm okay. Really."

"Have you taken any medication or tried to eat or drink?" Mia asked.

"A few sips of water and some Tylenol before I put the vegetables on my face."

She furrowed her brow. "How long have you felt nauseous?"

"That was the first time just now."

Heath shoved his fingers into his hair. Argh. This was so embarrassing. Who fell off ladders trying to paint a bedroom wall?

"How about ringing in your ears or double vision?"

He swallowed hard. "The room was spinning some, and I did hear ringing when I first came to, but it's gone."

"Good." Mia patted his arm. "You're doing great. A few more questions, then I'll be out of your hair."

The door opened and Gus stepped inside, bringing a wave of chilly air with him. He dusted the snow from his sweatshirt and toed off his boots. After closing the door, he crossed the room and handed Mia a gray backpack. "Here you go."

"Thanks." She smiled up at her husband.

Heath tried to look around and find Lexi, but moving his eyes that much physically hurt. He let them go closed.

"Will you let me clean up that wound?" Mia asked. "It will only sting for a few minutes. I have everything in my bag that I need to numb the area and stitch it."

Heath's breath hitched. Was it really that bad? "You don't need to do all of that."

"Please let us help you," Lexi said softly.

He opened his eyes and met her gaze. She hovered behind the sofa. "Mia's willing to patch you up. You don't have to go anywhere. Why won't you say yes?"

He swung his gaze toward Mia. "If that's what you think is best, go on and stitch me up. Please."

If he said yes to some first-aid treatment, then maybe he could avoid any more questions about his other symptoms. Because he definitely didn't want to tell Mia his health history. Hopefully he just had a concussion, but this ladder incident had planted doubt in his mind. What if his clumsiness was the first sign of Huntington's rearing its ugly head?

Chapter Eleven

Lexi's alarm woke her painfully early the next morning. She smacked the snooze button, then tugged the covers up to her chin. It was Monday and she didn't have any place she needed to be. No appointments. No clients. Nothing on the agenda other than another glorious hour of sleep. She burrowed deeper under the duvet.

Wait. There was something she'd said she'd do. What was it? An instant replay of yesterday's events spooled through her head. Coming home, hearing Scout's incessant barking and finding Heath with a head injury.

Oh, no. She sat straight up in bed. She'd promised to check on him during the night. He'd insisted that she absolutely would not sacrifice her sleep for him.

They'd compromised on an early-morning check-in. She threw back the duvet, peering at the clock on her nightstand as she swung her legs over the side of the bed. Five forty-five. She scrubbed her hands over her face, determined to wake up and pop next door. Part of her worried he'd try to work today, even though

Mia strongly advised that he stay home until his symptoms subsided.

She dressed quickly in gray leggings and a long-sleeved maternity shirt she'd plucked from the top of her clean laundry stack. Her standard wardrobe these days because it was one of the few outfits that still fit her.

After brushing her teeth, she twisted her hair into a messy bun. Breakfast could wait. She padded over to the front door, shrugged into her jacket, shoved her feet into her boots and headed next door. The spare key was still tucked in her jacket pocket from the night before.

A bitter wind greeted her when she stepped outside. The snow had stopped falling sometime during the night. She estimated about three to four inches sat on the ground. Her boots crunched across the fresh powder as she made her way down her driveway. Tucking her chin inside her jacket to shield at least part of her face from the cold air biting at her cheeks, she cut a straight path toward Heath's porch. It was way too early to barge in on him like this, but Mia had said it was wise to make sure his condition hadn't worsened. She reached for the doorbell but changed her mind. No sense getting Scout all riled up. She took the key from her pocket, unlocked the door, then quietly slipped inside.

"Hello? Heath?"

No answer. Not from the human, anyway.

Scout, on the other hand, spotted her. He whined and nudged at the door of his crate.

"I'll be right there." She shrugged out of her jacket, then slipped off her boots, shivering as her bare feet touched the cold entryway floor.

Scout's crate sat against the far wall in the space

that divided Heath's living area from his kitchen. The sweet dog had pressed his body against the door. He turned his soulful eyes her way.

"I see you, pal." She unlatched the wire door and took a step back. Scout pushed past her, trotted a lap around the kitchen island, then stopped and gave his body a thorough shake. The tags on his collar jangled together.

"Freedom feels good, doesn't it?" She filled his water bowl, then turned in a slow circle, looking around for his food. Snooping around didn't feel right, but feeding the dog was an essential task. Scout tracked her, his tail wagging expectantly.

She found a bin of dry dog food inside the pantry. "Let's start with a cup."

After she poured a scoop into his bowl, he dived in, happily crunching away. The smell of fresh paint still lingered in the air. Gus had said he'd cleaned up as best as he could in the room Heath had been painting. She wasn't about to wander down the hallway to check. Or risk approaching Heath's bedroom. That crossed way too many boundaries in their friendship. And she'd already trounced all over their boundaries a time or three. She wasn't about to let that happen again.

Except how could she know for certain that he was okay if she didn't see or speak to him?

Thankfully, a few minutes later Heath walked slowly into the kitchen.

"There you are." She smiled. "Good morning. How are you feeling?"

Heath palmed the back of his neck. He wore black sweats and a black-and-gray T-shirt with a team logo she'd never heard of. His hair stood up in tousled spikes.

An appealing scruff clung to his cheeks and angular jaw. She dragged her gaze to meet his.

"I've had better days." He frowned. "You didn't need to come over here. I'm fine."

She swallowed back a barbed comment about the shiner on his eye and the gnarly wound held together by a few stitches. He didn't look like he was in the mood for her jokes.

"Mia's orders, remember?" She pasted on a bright smile. "Head-injury victims are supposed to—"

"I'm not a victim." He winced and held up his palm.

Her breath hitched at his terse tone. Scout stopped eating and his head shot up. His nose twitched as he sniffed the air.

"I didn't mean to raise my voice," Heath said. "I'm sorry."

She fought to keep her tone gentle. "I'm truly only here to make doubly sure that you're all right. Can I get you anything? Coffee or toast?"

He shook his head. "I'm not really hungry."

"Are you sure you don't want to follow up with anyone at the clinic? Mia can make that happen, and I'd be more than happy to drive you over there."

The frost in his gaze sent chill bumps across her arms. "I'll take that as a no."

"Not interested." He shoved his hands in the pockets of his sweats. "Thanks for stopping by. I'll text if I need anything."

Wow, he was stubborn. "Splendid. You don't need to walk me out."

She hurried toward the door with Scout at her heels, whining. "I know, buddy. I'm sorry we can't hang out. Be good, okay?"

After a quick pat on the top of Scout's head, she put on her boots and jacket, then stepped out into the frigid morning. Her insides sparked with irritation.

"When I'm injured, he insists that I see a doctor immediately." She stormed down his driveway. "But when he gets hurt? It's like pulling teeth to get him to see someone."

Growling, she walked across her own driveway. It wasn't light enough for anyone to see or hear her. Not that she cared. She was too angry. "Heath Donovan, you are aggravating the tar out of me."

If it didn't hurt to stomp her healing foot, she'd take out her frustration on all three of her porch steps. Instead, she went inside and slammed the door. She took off her boots and her coat, then stalked down the hallway, climbed back into bed and yanked the covers over her head. She never should've gone over there. He was a grown man who evidently felt he could take care of himself. If he wanted to suffer alone, then good for him. She wasn't going to offer to help him anymore.

Boy, he'd messed that up.

Heath leaned both elbows on the kitchen counter, then gently rested his forehead on his arm. *Ouch.* He winced. The cut on his forehead was too tender for that kind of pressure. He slowly straightened and glanced around his kitchen. His empty, quiet kitchen.

Why had he run Lexi off like that? She'd only been trying to help.

Scout whined, his nails tapping out a steady rhythm as he crossed the kitchen and stood beside Heath. His tail thumped against the cabinet's wall. Heath rested his palm on the dog's head.

"I know, buddy. That was a disaster. I didn't handle her visit well at all, did I?"

Scout's dark eyes studied him. The tail wagging slowed to a pathetic droop.

"But what should I do differently? If I tell her about Huntington's running in my family, then she'll need to know that I might get sick. Or worse, pass it on to future generations. You weren't there, but she told Gus and Mia that she wanted more kids."

He sank onto the stool nearby. So this was a new low, trying to justify his behavior to his dog. Scout kept staring up at him, panting. Was he anxious that Lexi had been upset when she'd left?

Not that she'd said anything, because she was way too classy for that, but he'd seen the look in her eyes and the slump in her shoulders. Heath stroked the top of Scout's head. "Here's the thing, Scout. Why would a woman as amazing as Lexi want me to be anything more than a friend? She's about to become a single mom. If she wants to get married and have more kids, she needs somebody who is strong. Resilient. Not someone who will drag her down and die young."

Scout gave one last whine, then sank to the floor and rested his snout on his front legs. The long breath that left his lungs was almost as dramatic as Heath's.

"What am I going to do now?"

Okay, so he hadn't been kind. His reaction to her use of the word *victim* had been a bit over-the-top. Refusing to let her help him had been a ridiculous choice, because he did want breakfast and he probably had to see a doctor or physician assistant to get cleared to return to work.

Eyeing the coffee maker, he stood and walked slowly

toward the pantry. He set the bag of coffee and a loaf of bread on the counter. After filling the machine with water and fresh grounds, he hit the power button, then grabbed the bread to fix toast.

Lexi had been so sweet to offer to feed him and give him a ride to the clinic. Instead of graciously accepting her help, he'd pushed her away first. A classic self-preservation move. He knew this and he really didn't like that he'd done it, but wasn't he doing what was best for her in the long run?

The coffee maker gurgled and an appealing aroma filled the air. He should let Scout out before he ate anything. Heath walked to the back door. "Come on, boy. Let's go outside."

Scout followed him. After they stepped outside, the biting cold sent a shiver through Heath's body. He regretted not grabbing a coat. "Make this quick, Scout."

Hesitating, the dog stood on the patio slab and lowered his head, sniffing at the white snow covering the ground. Then he glanced up at Heath.

"It's fine. It's snow. I'm sure you'll have a blast. Go on." He motioned for Scout to explore the yard.

Scout's head swiveled. The errant curls on top fluttered in the wind. He took a few tentative steps, then stopped and sniffed the air.

Wouldn't that be something if his dog hated anything frozen touching his paws?

Scout took a few more steps before he broke into a trot. His paws left indentations in the snow as he trotted across the yard, stopping every few feet to gather up another mouthful of fresh powder. White clumps clung to his hair. What a mess that would be to deal with later. But despite his bleak circumstances, Heath couldn't help but smile and shake his head. Having Scout around made his challenges more palatable.

A pale blue sky painted with subtle streaks of orange and pink caught his attention. He wasn't a big fan of this biting wind and wouldn't stand out here for long without a coat, but the cold air stealing his breath made him stop and look around. He didn't like this version of himself very much. Not only had he likely hurt Lexi's feelings, but he'd also been quite rude.

Shame twisted his insides into hard knots.

The throbbing in his head that he'd experienced yesterday had lessened to a dull ache. And the nausea and double vision had vanished, too. He wasn't in any shape to go to work, but he also couldn't blame his concussion for his poor behavior. Standing there shivering in the wind, he glanced heavenward. "Lord, I haven't prayed in a very long time, and I'm sorry about that. Sorry for a lot of things, really. I think I need some help. I'm starting to make a mess of my life and I don't want to live this way. So what in the world do I do now?"

Lexi's first Thanksgiving in Hearts Bay had been far more enjoyable than she'd anticipated. She'd spent exactly two Thanksgivings away from her family back in Georgia. But only because she'd been with Beau's family in Indiana once, and she and Beau had spent their first Thanksgiving as newlyweds in Kansas when he'd been stationed at Fort Riley.

"Have you heard from anyone back in Georgia today?" Mama Madden, which Lexi had taken to affectionately calling her, studied her expectantly from across the Maddens' ginormous table.

"No, not yet." Lexi rested her silverware on the edge of her very clean plate, then reached for her napkin.

She'd checked her phone from time to time—okay, probably more than ten times already—to see if they'd called or sent a text message. Their perpetual silent treatment stung. She'd mailed her biological parents a card. Tried to be the bigger person and texted her mother early this morning, but unless there had been a new message sent while she was eating, she still hadn't heard anything. She scooted her chair back from the table and rubbed her taut stomach. Living so far from the Southern traditions she'd grown up with, she hadn't known what to expect for her first Thanksgiving in Alaska.

The traditional meal had been scrumptious. From the moist turkey and dressing the Maddens had served to the creamy garlic mashed potatoes, green beans topped with almonds and Mia's homemade rolls, Lexi had savored every delicious bite. Including the smoked salmon she'd sampled as an appetizer. Her very first experience with the Alaskan staple.

"Can I get you anything else?" Tess lifted Lexi's plate from the table. "We'll serve dessert soon. Just waiting on a few people to stop by."

More people? Lexi couldn't imagine who. Other than Eliana and Tate, who'd stayed in Idaho for Thanksgiving, she didn't know of any family members who weren't here.

She pushed to her feet. "Can I help clean up?"

"No, no," Tess said, patting her shoulder. "You're busy building a baby. Besides, we're considering you one of our special guests."

"Next year we'll put you to work," Rylee teased,

scooting past Lexi's chair with an empty casserole pan in her hands.

In the living room, the guys had gathered around the television to watch a football game. Their conversation, mostly reactions to the officials' calls and debates about which team had the best shot at the playoffs, filtered in.

Lexi smiled as Cameron played a game of peekaboo with Lucy at the other end of the table. Still strapped into her booster chair, Lucy clutched her sippy cup and giggled at her brother's antics. Lexi's thoughts turned to Beau. She had heard from his parents already. They'd sent a sweet selfie from the place they were staying in California. After they'd found the parts for their RV and the repairs were finished, they'd continued their adventure and made new friends. Which was how they'd ended up celebrating Thanksgiving at an RV park in central California.

A stone's throw from the beach, Beau's mama had said in her text.

Lexi had been prepared to shed a lot of tears today. Her first Thanksgiving in Alaska and her first without Beau. He'd passed away only seven months ago. But instead she felt incredibly content.

The doorbell rang.

"I'll get it." Rylee set another stack of dirty dishes on the counter by the dishwasher and left the room.

A few minutes later, she returned to the kitchen with Heath behind her.

Lexi's breath caught. Heath was the person they'd been waiting for?

His eyes, clouded with something that looked like embarrassment, locked on hers, then toggled toward the Madden ladies hovering in the kitchen. "Hi, every-one. Sorry I'm late."

"No problem." Tess gestured toward the empty chair across from Lexi. "Have a seat. We're getting ready to serve dessert."

He shrugged out of his jacket, draped it over his chair and sat down. "Hi, Lexi."

"Heath." Warmth climbed her neck. How had the room gotten so hot all of a sudden? "Happy Thanks-giving."

"Thanks. Same to you. Are you having a good day?"

"The best." She pasted on a bright smile. "You?"

He lifted one shoulder. "Yeah, it's been nice."

"Did you give Scout any turkey?"

"Absolutely not." His mouth curved up in a half smile. "My mom sent him another new toy, though."

"A turkey leg with a squeaker inside?" she dead-panned.

"Ha. No. A rope with knots on either end so we can play tug-of-war together."

"That should keep him entertained for ten or twelve minutes, right?"

Heath chuckled.

Wow. He looked handsome in his blue-and-gray-plaid button-down shirt. He was clean-shaven, which made his ruddy cheeks twice as appealing. The wound over his eyebrow had healed some. He looked much healthier than the last time they'd seen each other in his kitchen the day after he'd hit his head.

"How's the dog day care working out for Scout?"

She hadn't wanted to change their arrangement, but she'd become increasingly uncomfortable in these last weeks of her pregnancy. The mysterious pain in her hips was almost unbearable sometimes. She didn't have the energy to take Scout for their usual walks or play fetch in the yard. The sweet, rambunctious dog required more interaction than she could give, so she'd sent Heath a text message right after he'd gotten hurt and told him she couldn't care for Scout anymore.

Part of her had backed out because Heath had made her so angry, but she hadn't mentioned any of that. She didn't plan to bring up their last conversation right now, either. Not with so many people close by.

Heath's expression grew serious. "It's all right. Not his favorite place to go, but he stopped destroying stuff every time I bring him home, so that's progress."

Guilt pinched her insides. "Aw, poor buddy."

Heath looked like he wanted to say something else but Tess interrupted.

"Heath and Lexi, would you like pumpkin pie, pumpkin cheesecake or apple pie?" Tess stood at the kitchen counter, a pie server in hand and a stack of clean plates waiting on the counter next to the dessert options.

"You have to try the pumpkin cheesecake," Rylee said. "It's divine."

"I'll take a slice of that, then, please," Heath said.

"Same." Lexi reached for the pitcher of ice water and refilled her glass. "Can we get you something to drink?"

"Water, please." Heath clasped his hands together on the table in front of him. "Thank you."

She got up from the table, wincing as the now-familiar pain throbbed in both hips. *Only a couple more weeks.* Dr. Rasmussen had reassured her that the pain was a normal part of the process as her body adjusted to carrying a baby.

Sighing, she retrieved a clean glass from the cabinet beside the sink. Thankfully more people wandered in from the living room, including Annie and another older couple she assumed were Annie's parents. The woman looked remarkably like Annie, and the silver-haired gentleman wore a smile that matched his daughter's.

Lexi brought the glass to Heath. He accepted with a polite nod, and then he struck up a conversation with Annie's dad.

After she reclaimed her seat, she discreetly checked her phone. Still no messages from anyone in Georgia, not even her aunt and uncle. Disappointment settled in her chest. She splayed her fingers against her collarbone, as if the pressure could soothe the ache. Stave off a sense of looming panic.

She didn't regret moving here. Not at all. But this chasm between her and the people back in Georgia she'd always called her family, coupled with this weird dynamic in her friendship with Heath, made her feel uneasy. Did she have enough support? Was she equipped to bring a baby into the world as a single mom?

Chapter Twelve

The following Wednesday morning, Heath sat in the conference room at the police station, listening to the chief's briefing. Orca Island expected an influx of visitors next week, including multiple high school basketball teams in town to play in the holiday basketball tournament.

In the folding chair beside Heath, Kevin stirred a packet of sweetener into his disposable cup of coffee.

"We'll need additional patrols on—"

A sharp jolt interrupted the chief.

Heath flattened his palm on the table. "What was that?"

Everyone started talking at once, their voices rising. Heath eyed Kevin's coffee. The liquid on top rippled in concentric circles. The cup started dancing on the table.

"It's an earthquake!" Kevin stood and shoved his chair back. He tugged on Heath's uniform sleeve. "Get under the table."

Heath's stomach plummeted. He couldn't move. Couldn't think. Under the table? *Really?*

The clock mounted on the wall above the doorway

crashed to the floor. Next, the dry-erase markers on the whiteboard's tray and binders on the bookshelves fell.

The whole room swayed.

"Drop, cover and hold," the chief called out above the chaos. Panic washed through the room. Kevin's coffee tipped over, spilling a lake of liquid onto the table. It washed over the side in a mocha-brown waterfall. Heath leaped from his chair. The floor undulated beneath his work boots. He splayed his arms, desperate to keep his balance. Sidestepping the coffee, he got low, then wedged himself under the table beside his coworkers.

He hugged his knees to his chest. Throughout the police station, he heard more unknown items hitting the floor. How long did an earthquake last? Seconds? Surely not minutes. His mouth ran dry, envisioning the damage caused by a catastrophic tremor.

"Everyone sit tight. We'll get through this." The chief's deep voice betrayed his concern.

A loud crash echoed through the room.

"What was that?" Kevin's eyes grew wide. "The windows?"

Adrenaline surged through Heath's veins. An odor of sweat and coffee filled the confined space as they all huddled shoulder to shoulder. The room kept rolling and shaking. Kelsey, the station's administrative assistant, had been in the room when the earthquake started. Now she sat nearby, reciting the Lord's Prayer. Tears glistened on her pink cheeks.

His mind spun, serving up an image of Lexi, smiling at him from across the Maddens' table at Thanksgiving. Was she alone? Did she know to take cover and hold, like the chief had instructed them? Did people who grew up in the South know what to do in an earth-quake? The questions raced through his head like an elite runner, sprinting around a track. A fresh wave of panic squeezed the air from his lungs.

At last the shaking stopped. Everything was ee-rily quiet.

"Thank You, Lord," he whispered.

Kelsey reached over and squeezed his forearm. Her hand was ice-cold.

"Amen." Her smile wobbled. Moisture clung to her lashes. "We made it."

"All right, people, listen up." The chief, still sitting under the table, cupped his hands around his mouth to project his voice. "We can expect tsunami warn-ing sirens shortly. Residents will have approximately ninety minutes to get to higher ground before a tidal wave potentially reaches our community."

Heath's heart hammered. A *tsunami*?

"Remember, this is an island," the chief continued. "We can only move to higher ground. There's no way to get to the mainland in time. Direct anyone you en-counter to drive toward the high school or the parking lot near the Mount Larsen trailhead. Let's dispatch in teams of two. Grab a disaster preparedness kit on your way out. Those are the red duffel bags in the closet by the back doors. Above all, be safe."

"Let's go." Kevin tapped Heath's knee. "It's you and me, bro. I've got a chain saw in my truck."

"A chain saw?" Heath scrambled after him. "What for?"

"Downed trees, my man." Kevin was one of the first to climb out from under the table. He righted two folding chairs that had been knocked over. "Let's grab those bags and get to work."

Heath waited, letting Kelsey go first. Once he was out from under the table, he quickly scanned the room. Officers all around him did the same.

"We need to check on my next-door neighbor," Heath said, sidestepping more binders and a few dry-erase markers that had rolled across the room. He followed Kevin toward the door. "She's super pregnant. Lives alone. I'm worried about her."

"That can be our first stop," Kevin said. "Assuming we can get to your neighborhood."

Heath's steps faltered. "Why couldn't we?"

"Downed power lines, tree limbs, roads cracked in half," Kevin called over his shoulder as he strode down the hallway toward the closet that housed the emergency preparedness kits. "Who knows what we'll find when we get out there."

A shiver danced down his spine. Those scenarios all sounded less terrifying than a massive tidal wave overtaking the island. Well, except for the part about roads cracked in half. He'd seen plenty of those pictures online and in the news after previous earthquakes. This was the first significant earthquake he'd ever experienced. Sure, there had been the occasional tremor during his childhood in Eastern Washington, but never anything like this. What if his neighborhood wasn't accessible? What if Lexi and everyone else had to stay in their houses because they couldn't drive to higher ground?

His stomach twisted. *No.* He couldn't let that happen.

With their red duffel bags in hand, Heath and Kevin

hurried out the back door of the police station and into the parking lot. A piercing siren filled the air.

"What is that?" Heath hunched his shoulders.

"Tsunami warning," Kevin yelled. He gestured toward his SUV parked nearby. "We've got to go. The clock's ticking. Chief said less than ninety minutes, remember?"

Oh, he remembered. As he jogged toward Kevin's vehicle, the bag bouncing against his leg, he silently launched another prayer toward heaven.

Clear a path for us, Lord. Please.

They had to find a way to help Lexi and any other people they encountered. And what about Scout? The poor dog had probably sensed danger. Was he safe at the kennel? How were they supposed to evacuate pets and people? Sweat slicked his skin. More adrenaline zipped through his veins. Heath climbed into the passenger seat in Kevin's truck, then pulled his phone from his pocket. A text message from Patti, the kennel owner, waited for him.

Scout is safe. We're on our way to the high school. Hope to see you there.

A relieved breath left his lungs. Good. Scout was okay. Now he had to get to Lexi.

The mournful wail of that bizarre siren outside had propelled Lexi into action. She didn't know what it meant. But the power was out and she'd misplaced her phone. Maybe that sound was meant to alert the island that an earthquake had happened. Although how someone could've missed it was beyond her. She'd heard that Alaskans grew accustomed to experiencing frequent small earthquakes. This one had hardly been small, though.

In the living room, she shoved her hand between the sofa cushions. The gray morning light coming through her window didn't give her much to work with. It took some effort, but she sank to her knees and checked under the sofa, too. She'd fallen asleep here watching a movie last night. Her phone had to be around here somewhere.

Maybe she'd left it on the kitchen counter while she made breakfast. Discomfort throbbed low in her abdomen as she pushed to her feet and walked into the kitchen. Fragments of a broken plate littered the floor. She pulled the broom from the closet and started sweeping up the mess.

Another bizarre tremor shimmied through her house. *Again?*

She dropped the broom and clutched the edge of the kitchen counter with both hands. A bolt of terror zipped through her. Less than an hour ago, an earthquake had rocked her house for what seemed like an eternity. Was this one of those aftershocks?

Glasses and dishes in her kitchen cabinets rattled. The floor shook beneath her feet.

"Lord, please make it stop."

Low bands of tension tightened across her belly and wrapped around to her back.

Oh, *no.*

The room stopped shaking, but the siren kept right on wailing.

With the pain in her lower back growing more pronounced, she slowly bent down to pick up the broom.

An alarming sound blared from her phone. Startled, she straightened and followed the sound to her dining room table. She found the device under a magazine she'd been reading earlier. A man's urgent voice broadcast from the speaker.

"From the Tsunami Warning Service, an earthquake measured at 7.3 on the Richter scale occurred at 9:23 a.m. 170 miles southwest of Orca Island. A tsunami warning has been issued. All residents should seek higher ground immediately."

Lexi's breath locked in her lungs. Seek higher ground? A tsunami?

"This isn't happening," she whispered. Between the blaring siren outside and the warning on her phone, she was about to launch into a full-on freak-out. She had to reach somebody in the Madden family. They'd know what to do. The pain and discomfort in her body made her nervous. Was this how early stages of labor felt? She'd read that chapter in her book a few times, but now she wasn't sure her symptoms lined up with what she'd read about.

The siren and the warning and her fear all swirled together, making rational thought a challenge. She couldn't quite wrap her mind around the concept of a massive tidal wave. It was too frightening to think about, really. And what was she supposed to pack? Her hospital bag had been ready to go for a week. Somehow that hardly seemed adequate now, especially if she'd have to spend days or even weeks in an emergency shelter.

Panic careened through her system like a champion bobsledder on a high-stakes course. So she was possibly in labor after an earthquake on an island in the middle of the ocean expecting a giant wave to hit soon. And they didn't have electricity.

Super.

"Lord, please. I really need help," she whispered. Hot tears stung the backs of her eyes.

Evacuating her home wasn't how she'd wanted to give birth. Although her mother had given birth in the middle of a natural disaster on this very island. How ironic.

She swept the broken dish into a pile, leaned the broom against the counter and went in search of shoes. Her feet were so swollen only a pair of canvas sneakers fit. She shoved them on, then retrieved a flashlight from her nightstand drawer.

"Please work." She held her breath, then clicked the power button. A beautiful beam of light illuminated her bedroom floor. As she turned toward the closet to get her hospital bag, suddenly an impressive amount of water saturated her plaid pajamas, then trickled down her leg.

"No, no, no. We're not doing this. Not like this, anyway."

Emotion tightened her throat. "Don't panic."

A contraction wrapped around her belly and squeezed. The pain in her lower back made her suck in a sharp breath. Wait. She was supposed to time all this, right? First things first. She changed into clean, dry clothes, then grabbed her bag. A loud knocking sound outside caught her attention. Someone was at the door.

"Help is here. Yes! Thank You, Lord."

She needed help from someone. Anyone. Her family. A firefighter. Heath. Almost anybody would do at this point. Because she could not give birth alone in this house.

She left her room and made her way toward the front door. Three framed photographs she'd hung in the hall last week had fallen. Bits of broken glass spilled across the floor.

"Not going to think about it. I can't think about it. These are all just things."

In the living room she halted her steps at the sight of her and Beau's wedding photo on the ground. Oh, no. She leaned over and picked it up, carefully avoiding more broken glass. The picture wasn't damaged. Only the glass had shattered.

"Sorry, baby." She blinked back another wave of tears and set the frame on the side table. A smaller, more portable photo of her and Beau had already been tucked deep inside her bag. A little something to carry with her as she delivered their baby.

The knocking on the door grew louder. "Lexi!"

Heath.

Relief flooded through her. She hurried to the door as quickly as she could, sidestepping books that had landed on the floor and another piece of framework that had fallen from the wall. She yanked open the door.

Heath stood on her porch in his police officer uniform. Concern was etched on his features. "Are you all right?"

"Yes. No. I—I don't know."

"We need to go." He gestured to the bag in her hand. "Is everything you need in there?"

"Define *everything*," she said through gritted teeth, pressing her free hand to the small of her back.

Heath's eyes widened. "What's wrong?"

"Would now be a good time to mention that I think my water broke and my contractions are less than five minutes apart?" She groaned. "Oh, Mylanta, this is really starting to hurt."

"Okay, okay." Heath's Adam's apple bobbed up and down. "Kevin is right outside with his vehicle. We need to get to the high school. It's our emergency shelter."

"Don't you mean the *hospital*?"

Heath scrubbed his fingers along his jaw, hesitating. "We're directing everyone to the high school. It's considered higher ground, which is the safest place to be right now. It's going to be fine."

"There's a massive wave coming," she said, raising her voice. "That's the opposite of fine."

"Is there anything else you want me to grab before we go?"

She turned in a slow circle, battling back more tears and the desperate urge to scream. "Maybe some towels from the linen closet?"

"I'll get the towels. Stay here." He brushed past her. Glass crunched under his boots as he hurried down the hall. Another contraction nearly took her down. She tried to pace, then stopped and forced herself to breathe.

Heath returned with a stack of towels. Those were some of her favorites, but she wasn't going to complain. This was not the time to be picky. She needed medical attention. The health and safety of herself and her baby were really what mattered. Not a bunch of terry cloth that could be replaced.

"Where's Scout?" she asked, following him out onto the porch.

"He's already on his way to the shelter with Patti, the woman who runs the dog day care."

"Oh, good. He'll be great company for whoever is at the shelter with us."

Heath gave her a tender smile. "Agreed."

She tried to smile back, but it came out more like a grimace. Another intense contraction tightened her muscles. Pain shot down her legs. "We'd better get going. I really don't want to give birth in my front yard. Or on the side of the road somewhere."

"Come on. I'll help you get in Kevin's SUV." He opened the passenger door for her. "Can you get in?"

She bit her lip and eyed the step up into the cab. Heath took her bag from her hand. "One second and I'll help."

"Here, I'll put your things in the back. Heath, you focus on helping Lexi." Kevin got out of the truck and circled around the front. He took the towels and her bag.

Heath offered his hand. She gladly reached for it, drawing strength from his warm grasp. It took some maneuvering, but she finally got inside the vehicle. He gently closed the door, then climbed in the middle row behind her.

The tsunami siren wailed again. Her pulse sped. Never in a million years would she have imagined that this could happen. Heath reached over the seat and gently squeezed her shoulder.

"Lexi, I promise we're going to get through this. Kevin will take us to the high school, and we'll find Mia or Dr. Rasmussen or somebody to help you deliver a healthy baby. Everything's going to be fine."

"I hope you're right," she whispered, staring straight ahead. As Kevin backed out of her driveway, she gave her house one last look. What was she going to do if everything she'd saved and stockpiled for the baby was washed away?

* * *

How could one tiny human who was only hours old steal his heart so quickly?

Heath stared in awe at Lexi's newborn baby girl swaddled in his arms. She slept with her little Cupid's bow of a mouth hanging open. Wisps of dark hair peeked from the fold of her pink knit hat, and the nurse who'd assisted Lexi had wrapped the baby in a white blanket with a pink-and-blue heart pattern. From her long dark eyelashes and smooth, round cheeks to the miniature little fingers clutching the edge of the blanket, he couldn't get over the fact that she was here.

Lexi reclined on a cot, propped up with pillows. The wall of windows above her head overlooked Hearts Bay. She offered him a tired smile. "What do you think?"

"She's perfect." Heath cleared the emotion wedged in his throat. "Congratulations."

Lexi brushed a strand of hair from her flushed face. "Thank you."

He didn't want to move. Barely wanted to breathe, for fear of disturbing her. "Have you decided on a name yet?"

Her smile grew wider. "I have. Are you ready?"

"Tell me."

"This is Molly Jo Thomas."

"I love it," Heath said. "She looks like a Molly Jo."

Lexi chuckled. "Really? Have you met a lot of babies named Molly Jo in your life?"

"No, she's the first one. I'm just saying I think it fits. Nicely done."

"I'm glad you like it." Lexi's expression sobered. "I'm naming her after Beau's mother and grandmother. That's sort of a Southern thing, but it's what he would've wanted."

"Are Beau's mother and grandmother still living?"

"They are. I can't wait to tell them the news." She wrinkled her nose. "They're going to flip when I tell them the whole story. By the way, I couldn't have made it here without you and Kevin. Please tell him thank you."

"Of course." Heath glanced around the classroom. Desks had been pushed aside and chairs had been stacked neatly to make room for Dr. Rasmussen, Mia and several other staff members from the hospital who'd worked quickly to prepare for an emergency childbirth.

Lexi had delivered her baby less than an hour after Kevin and Heath had helped her inside. The emergency management team who'd converted the high school into a shelter had carved out zones in the building to meet the various needs of the residents who'd streamed through the doors.

"I still can't believe we didn't get a tsunami." Lexi shook her head, then reached for her bottle of water. "What a tremendous blessing."

"Yeah, we're very fortunate," Heath said. "When I went to get you some water, the women serving food gave me an update. Other parts of coastal Alaska, especially in the southeast, might still be affected, but we're in the clear."

Lexi's shoulders sagged. She blew out a breath. "I'm sorry for anybody else who has to deal with evacuating, not to mention a tidal wave. But selfishly, I'm grateful we're safe. How soon before we'll know about the houses in our neighborhood?"

"I haven't been outside to look around yet." Heath tipped his head toward the windows. "The view from here is great, but I can't see certain parts of the island. Some other guys chatting out in the gym said there's flooding in the buildings closest to the water, and several boats have been damaged."

"Oh, dear." Lexi frowned. "I'm guessing there's quite a bit of debris to be cleaned up."

Molly Jo stirred in his arms. Her flawless brow pinched and her eyelids fluttered. He stood still, his pulse thrumming. The instant she cried, he fully intended to hand her over to Lexi. He was stalling. Trying in vain to avoid the unavoidable. Because the time had come for him to tell Lexi everything.

The dreaded ninety minutes had passed. No tidal wave had ever come. The siren had stopped. Now they all waited, trying to be patient, until the weather service issued the blessing to return to their homes and businesses.

Molly Jo settled and released a contented sigh.

"I'm going to give her back before she wakes up," Heath said.

"No problem." Lexi received her baby, tucking her gently into the crook of her elbow, like she'd done it a thousand times.

Heath couldn't help but stare. He hated that he couldn't stay and be a part of helping Lexi get settled back at her house. His mouth went dry. He shot a glance toward the door. If he didn't hurry up and say what he needed to say, Mia or the doctor or somebody would be by to check on Lexi and the baby. Then he'd have to wait until they were alone again.

He couldn't put this off any longer.

The hum of conversation and laughter of kids playing an impromptu game of tag in the gym down the hall filtered through the air. He grimaced. The smell of coffee and damp clothing didn't make for an aesthetically pleasing environment, but at least they were all safe.

Lexi glanced up at him. Her eyes clouded. "Are you okay?"

He shook his head, then jammed his hands in the pockets of his uniform. "There's something I need to tell you."

"All right." She bit her lip.

He rocked back on his heels. Fear squeezed the air from his lungs. "From that first day that Scout knocked you over and made you spill those flowers, I wanted to get to know you better."

Her mouth tipped up in a cautious half smile. "Aw, that's so sweet."

"But there's something that I have to tell you. The truth is, I can't be a part of your life. Not now. Really not ever."

Pain flashed in her eyes. "What are you saying, Heath?"

Hesitating, he palmed the back of his neck and swallowed hard. "I have a family history of Huntington's disease. It's what killed my dad. I haven't developed symptoms yet, at least any that are outwardly visible. And…I don't want to do any kind of testing to find out if I will."

"But you can't be sure, right?"

"Here's what I do know for sure," he said, his voice thick with emotion. "You have a brand-new, beautiful baby girl. I know you hope to complete your family with more children and—"

"There are lots of ways to grow a family. If you're

implying that you can't be that guy, I think you're getting ahead of yourself."

Her reaction flustered him. Didn't she understand? Maybe she didn't realize that there wasn't a cure for this horrific disease. As much as it hurt to tell her everything, he couldn't stop now.

"You have your whole life ahead of you, Lexi. I'm not going to stand in your way. Not when you've already endured so much loss."

A mournful look glistened in her eyes. "Are you serious?"

His legs itched to run. He wanted to get out of here. But he couldn't. Oh, he should've told her the truth weeks ago. Maybe even months.

"I know the timing really stinks here, but surviving a natural disaster, witnessing emergency childbirth and meeting Molly Jo has made me realize that I just can't keep this secret any longer. And I also can't put you in a position to make an impossible choice. You—"

"Hold on," Lexi interrupted, grimacing as she shifted her weight on the cot. "You haven't put me in a position to make any choice at all. You're deciding for me. You just said that because you might develop symptoms of a fatal disease or you're a possible carrier for this condition, you'd rather be alone than face an uncertain future with me? Am I hearing you correctly?"

Her voice had grown progressively louder with every sentence. A volunteer who'd stepped into the room with a tray of food immediately turned around and left.

Molly Jo stirred in her arms. Lexi glanced down and gently adjusted the baby's blanket. Then her gaze met his again. The pain reflected in her eyes stabbed him in the heart.

"I never meant to hurt you."

"Oh, please. You absolutely meant to hurt me. Otherwise you would've told me this sooner. Like after we kissed? You're being a coward, Heath Donovan."

He winced and took a step back. "I'm sorry that you feel that way. I don't know what else to say. Congrats again on delivering a beautiful, healthy baby girl. You're an incredibly brave woman and I know you're going to be a great mom."

He turned and strode out of the room before she said anything else that might persuade him to change his mind. There. He'd done it. He'd mustered the courage and told her everything. So why did he feel a thousand percent worse?

Chapter Thirteen

"I can't believe he bailed on you like that," Rylee said, standing in the middle of Lexi's living room. She swayed side to side with a fussy Molly Jo in her arms. There had been a lot of crying today. Nothing Lexi had done seemed to soothe her baby girl. Thankfully, Tess, Mia and Rylee had come to her rescue.

"It's not great timing." Lexi lifted the lid on another box of Christmas decorations Tess had just hauled in from the garage. "But I understand his perspective now that I've had a couple of weeks to think and do research online. He's afraid he has the genetic makeup to develop symptoms of a fatal disease."

"But he won't know for sure unless he gets some kind of testing, right?" Tess carried a plate of freshly decorated Christmas sugar cookies in from the kitchen.

"I don't fully understand that part," Lexi admitted. She stacked the containers of shiny silver and red balls neatly on the floor. "I shouldn't have called him a coward, though. What if his decision to protect me was actually quite noble?"

Rylee rolled her eyes. "It was not noble. He's being a big chicken."

Lexi frowned. "I thought we were going to watch one of those sweet made-for-TV holiday movies?"

Although she wasn't really in the mood for a feel-good romantic flick, she also didn't have the emotional energy to rehash every single thing that Heath had said to her. The appealing scent of her new Sitka spruce Christmas tree filled the air. Now, if she could just find the box with the lights, then she could get started decorating. Molly Jo would be hungry soon, so Lexi wanted to enjoy the ladies' company and make the most of their time together.

"Mia, what do you think?" Rylee turned to where Mia sat on the sofa, scrolling through the channels with Lexi's remote control. "Why can't Heath just get tested? Then he'd know for sure."

Mia forced a bright smile. Her emerald gaze toggled between Rylee and Lexi. "Who wants a cookie? Rylee, I'll let you pick the movie."

Lexi chuckled. "Way to dodge the question."

Mia's smile faded. "Heath's not my patient and I'm not an expert."

"But we went through something similar with Mom and her aplastic anemia. Isn't there some overlap in the genetic sciency stuff?" Tess gestured with her hand before plucking a cookie from the plate.

"Yeah, Mia, you're a medical professional and we rely on you for useful information," Rylee said. "Even though he's not your patient, he's really no one's patient since he won't see a doctor about this. You must have an opinion on the best course of action."

Molly Jo's fussiness accelerated to a full-blown newborn howl.

"Oh, dear." Rylee glanced down at her red-faced niece. "Next suggestion, please? My baby-whispering skills need some work."

"Do you have one of those vibrating bouncy seats?" Mia asked. "I thought I saw one around here."

"It's in her bedroom, although I don't know if I put the batteries in yet."

"I'm on it," Tess said around a mouthful of cookie. She dusted her fingertips on a napkin, then strode down the hall.

Mia set the remote down without selecting a movie. "Here's what I've learned so far about Huntington's. It's rare, impossible to cure, and once a person receives a diagnosis, their decline can be quite rapid."

Rylee shifted Molly Jo to her shoulder and gently patted her backside.

"I understand why you think people should find out if they're carriers or if they have a chance of developing the disease," Mia continued. "But some people feel that isn't necessary. They'd rather not know."

"I've read that sometimes people don't do any kind of testing and they just wait until they develop symptoms," Lexi added.

"The important thing to remember is that everybody gets to make their own decision." Mia gave Rylee the side-eye. "Even if we don't agree with their perspective."

"I'm allowed to have an opinion," Rylee said, bending and straightening her knees. Molly Jo cried harder. "Please remember that I'm Team Lexi all the way."

"Thank you," Lexi said. "I know you are and I appreciate your concern. Would you like me to take the baby? She might be hungry."

"Please."

Rylee crossed the room and handed Molly Jo over.

"Come here, sweet pumpkin." She cradled her daughter in her arms, breathing in the sweet scent of the gentle soap she'd used to bathe her earlier. Settling into the rocker she'd arranged in the corner of the living room, she pulled a light blanket from the tufted footrest and draped it over her shoulder.

As she nursed Molly Jo, Tess, Mia and Rylee chatted about their holiday plans and unboxed the rest of Lexi's Christmas decorations.

"Oh, this is precious." Mia held up an ornament that Lexi had set on the coffee table. "Did you just get this?"

Lexi nodded. "It's from Beau's parents."

The ornament featured an oval picture frame and three tiny silver blocks dangling in a row. Each block had a capital letter in it. A nod to the ABCs. After the *C*, a small rectangular sign featured the words *Baby's First Christmas*. Lexi couldn't wait to add the ornament to her tree. Even though she had no earthly idea how she'd get a picture made of Molly Jo that was small enough to put inside the frame.

They'd abandoned their plans to watch a movie. Rylee streamed popular Christmas music from her phone instead. An icy rain pelted the window outside. Another storm had rolled in. She wasn't about to let the gloomy weather or rehashing Heath's words ruin her festive mood. Beau's parents had found inexpensive airline tickets for mid-January and they'd made plans to come to Hearts Bay. So now she and Molly Jo had Christmas, New Year's and a visit from their first out-of-town guests to look forward to.

If she was honest, Heath's absence had left a big old gaping crater in her life. She'd tried convincing herself that her attraction toward him wasn't genuine, but her feelings had only grown stronger. Then there was the guilt. Beau hadn't been gone long. How could she possibly fall in love again so soon? Caring for a newborn had given her plenty of time while she nursed to think and pray. Beau's death was a tragedy. Nothing could bring him back. Part of her would always love him, and she'd tell Molly Jo dozens of stories about her amazing daddy. But he wouldn't want her and Molly Jo to remain alone forever.

Not that any of her thoughts and feelings about Heath could change his mind. He'd made his choice and she'd have to learn to live with that. She certainly wasn't going to march next door and try to convince him that he needed her. If they were meant to be, the Lord would make a way.

"Dude, you're an idiot." Reid picked up a pillow from Heath's sofa and tossed it at him. Heath caught it before it pegged him in the head. Or smacked into the fireplace behind him.

"What's that supposed to mean?"

Reid's blue eyes narrowed. "Did I stutter? You heard me. I can't believe you told a woman she couldn't be part of your life because you *might* have a disease."

Man, his brother didn't mince words. He clutched a pillow with both hands until his knuckles turned white and drew a calming breath. "She has a new baby. Plus, she lost her husband already. She doesn't need to lose a second one."

"Did you give her any say in the matter?"

Heath pressed his lips into a flat line. Funny thing, that was the same logic that Lexi had used.

"I'll take that as a no," Reid said. "When you develop symptoms, then you can start telling people that this disease is impacting your life."

Mom came into the room, her brow furrowed. She sat down on the sofa and placed her hand on Reid's arm. "Honey, let's try to empathize with his perspective."

"I did. He told a beautiful woman who just survived an earthquake and had a baby that he couldn't be part of her life because he might die."

Heath regretted ever telling his brother about his next-door neighbor. Yesterday Reid had spotted her unloading groceries from her car and started in with all kinds of questions.

"We're all going to die, Heath. There's a one hundred percent guarantee on—"

"Reid." His mom's tone, even though they were adults, indicated she meant business. "Give him a minute to explain himself."

Reid sat back against the sofa cushions and linked his arms across his chest, still glowering.

Heath's gaze swung to Mom. "There's not much else I can say. Lexi's a lovely person and I only want what's best for her."

She nodded. "I understand."

"You look like you have something more on your mind."

"I'm concerned." Mom tugged at a loose thread on

the seam of her jeans. "You've lived on this island for six months now and your lifestyle is still so isolated."

"What?" Heath scoffed. "I'm not—"

She held up one finger to silence him.

Reid smirked.

It was Heath's turn to pin him with an icy glare.

"I know you have a good job," Mom continued. "And surviving an earthquake has certainly helped you bond with others in the community. But now you're telling us that you've severed a relationship with a lovely woman before it's even gotten off the ground."

Heath tipped his head back and stifled a groan. "Did you hear the part about her being a widowed single mom with a newborn?"

"I did. She sounds like a remarkable young woman. The kind of person who could weather just about anything that life throws at her."

"Like a progressively fatal disease?" Reid added, pressing his fingertip to his scruffy chin.

Anger simmered low in Heath's gut. He intentionally looked away. If Reid didn't back off, they were going to wrestle before the day was over.

"I understand that you're looking out for her and her best interests, but if she cares deeply for you, then shouldn't she have a say in what happens next?"

"All right, all right," Heath said. "I get the message."

Mom's expression brightened. "So you'll talk to her, then?"

"No, that's not what I meant. I'm saying I heard you. By the way, that's exactly what she said. Oh, and she told me that I was being selfish and behaving like a coward."

"Duh," Reid said.

Heath chucked the pillow back at his brother.

Reid laughed and plucked it out of the air.

"Boys, that's enough. You're behaving like children." Mom snatched the pillow and gave them both her most withering look. "I'm sorry that you've lost your father, and that you're both living in fear of your health declining. But that is no way to honor his memory. A life that he lived well. We are blessed that we had him as long as we did."

Emotion clogged Heath's throat. He didn't want to admit that she was right. They had made some great memories as a family. He still wished that there had been more time to enjoy the activities Dad had loved.

Mom angled her body slightly toward Reid. "I hate that you've developed a couple of symptoms. Only time will tell what that means for you."

Heath's stomach twisted. They'd spent a whole week together without discussing the horrid disease. Now Reid refused to look at him. Yes, Reid had lost his job because of mistakes he'd made with the forklift in the warehouse, and Heath had noticed the tremor in his brother's arm, but that didn't mean he had Huntington's.

Did it?

And when would they know for sure?

"No matter what happens, I'm here for both of you, whether you develop Huntington's or not. Caring for your father was one of the most humbling and beautiful experiences of my life. I wouldn't trade it for anything because it blessed me and grew my faith in unexpected ways."

Heath pressed the heels of his hands to his eyes. What had he done? He didn't want to admit that Reid was right. But Mom's words moved him. Silence filled the room. It was way too quiet. He swiped his fingers quickly across his cheeks, then cleared his throat and looked around.

"Have you guys seen Scout?"

His mom shifted, craning her neck to check behind the sofa. "Not recently. I assumed he was asleep somewhere."

Uh-oh.

"We were playing fetch earlier," Reid said. "Then I let him out because he was scratching at the back door. I thought you had that nice new fence."

Reid stood and crossed to the living room window.

Heath moved toward the back door. He shrugged into his jacket and quickly put his sneakers on.

Reid chuckled. "Maybe he jumped over."

"I hope not."

Outside, a light rain pattered his face. He called for Scout.

A chickadee perched on top of the fence chirped back. The trees on the backside of his fence swayed, their branches dancing in the wind.

He walked through the yard. Evidence of dirt dug up near the back fence caught his eye. Scout had been digging here recently, but not enough of a hole to get through. He was about to go inside when he noticed the gate at the side of the house between his yard and Lexi's was open.

That rascal.

Heath walked back to his patio and popped his head in the back door. "The gate's open. I'm going to look for him."

"Do you need help?" Mom stood at the kitchen counter, stirring honey into her hot tea.

"No, thanks. I'm pretty sure I know where to find him."

Scout the matchmaker. Heath shook his head as he crossed the yard toward Lexi's place. Leave it to his headstrong, mischievous Goldendoodle to bring him and Lexi face-to-face again.

"Oh, my. I'm so happy to see you, sweet boy." Lexi laughed, squeezing her eyes shut as Scout licked her face. She buried her fingers in the soft hair on the sides of his big head and showered him with affection.

"Okay, okay." Putting some space between his mouth and her face, she tried to stand up. His tail wagged hard, thwacking against the glass on her back door. "I've missed you. How was your Christmas?"

Scout sneaked in one last sloppy lick on her chin, then darted past her and zoomed around the kitchen, leaving a trail of muddy paw prints.

But she didn't even care.

He circled the kitchen table and came to a halt when he found Molly Jo sound asleep in the bouncy seat.

"Oh, yeah, a few things have changed around here." Lexi quickly grabbed a folded onesie off the stack of clean laundry in the middle of the table. "Here. I want you to meet someone."

She held out the onesie and let Scout sniff it. He stood completely still, except for his big black nose, working double-time to take in this new scent. Then his tail started to wag again.

"This is Molly Jo," Lexi said.

Scout dipped his head and gently licked Molly Jo's head.

Molly Jo's little forehead crinkled but she didn't wake up.

Emotion clogged Lexi's throat. Oh, brother. Was she

seriously going to cry about a dog licking her baby's head? Wasn't she supposed to worry about germs and protecting her child from such an exuberant animal?

Except Scout was so sweet. She truly wasn't worried. He whined and turned in a circle, then curled up on the kitchen floor beside the bouncy seat. He rested his snout on his paws and stared up at her.

"Yes, I know. I've missed you, too, and you are such a good boy. I'm sorry we haven't been able to see each other very much."

A subtle knock rapped on her sliding glass door. Lexi turned around.

Heath stood on the other side, uncertainty written in his eyes. He wore a dark blue jacket layered over a gray shirt, faded jeans and sneakers. Her gaze lingered on the stubble clinging to his strong jaw.

Wow, he looked handsome. Her heart turned pirouettes. She wasn't quite ready for him to know how much she'd missed him, though. She glanced back at the dog. "Look who's here, Scout."

The dog tracked her movement but made zero effort to stand up and go to the door.

"Don't worry. I've got this." Lexi crossed the kitchen and opened the door. "Hi."

"Hi." He scraped his shoes against the doormat. "I see my dog is making himself at home."

"Come on in." Lexi stepped back. "He just met Molly Jo."

"Yeah? How'd that go?"

"Great. He was so gentle and sweet. Made me a little emotional."

Heath stepped inside and closed the door, then faced her. His eyes roamed her face. "Merry Christmas."

"Merry Christmas." She offered what she hoped was a cheery smile. "Did you have a nice holiday?"

He nodded. "It was nice. My brother and my mom are visiting. How about you?"

Oh, this small talk was so painful. She clasped her hands in front of her, inwardly regretting that she wore her oldest pair of yoga pants and a faded T-shirt from college that had definitely seen better days.

"I didn't get much sleep, but that's to be expected. The Maddens were very good to me, though. I'm super grateful."

His expression sobered. "Do you have a few minutes? I mean, I did come by to get my dog, but there are also some things I'd like to say."

Lexi hesitated, then checked on Molly Jo. "I can talk until she wakes up."

"Yeah, of course. I just wanted to say that I'm so very sorry. You were right. I was being a selfish coward."

She winced. "I could've phrased that differently. I'm sure you're only doing what you believe is right."

His brow scrunched together. "No, I did what was easiest for me."

Oh. A ribbon of hope twirled inside. Scout whined, then stood and walked toward them. He stopped beside Lexi. She pressed her hand to the top of his head. Yes, he was Heath's pet, but she really appreciated his comforting presence right now.

"I was just talking with my mom and my brother. They told me some things that I needed to hear."

"Such as?"

"Lexi." Heath moved closer and reached for her hands. She let him hold on to her, grateful for the warmth of his fingers twined through hers. "I am so sorry, not only for what I said to you but the way I've behaved. I pushed you away repeatedly, even when you were sweet and kind and generous. You'll never know how much I regret that. Will you please forgive me?"

"I forgive you." She angled her head to one side. His eyes were the most incredible shade of blue. She couldn't look away. "Please know that I will do whatever I can to support and encourage you. The decision to get genetic testing done isn't mine alone to make. I'll try to be brave and face the uncertainty right along with you, because I can't possibly know what it's like to be in your position."

Wow, where had all that come from? Had to be a God thing, granting her the words, because she hadn't felt that generous or that brave about Heath's health situation before now.

He caressed the back of her hand with his thumb, sending a delightful tingle up her arm. "So, you envision us having a future together?"

She couldn't stop a smile. "Absolutely."

"I have a confession."

Oh, no. Her smile evaporated. "I'm ready."

"I've wanted to be so much more than your friend ever since we went hiking. I was just too scared to admit it."

"Well, that's good to know, because I've been quite smitten ever since you brought me lemonade at Maverick's, then drove me home."

His blue eyes darkened to a shade of even more appealing indigo. "I love you, Lexi."

"I love you, too," she whispered.

His eyes dipped to her lips. "Mind if I kiss you?"

She pressed up on her tiptoes. "Don't make me wait another second."

He let go of her hands, but only so he could cradle her face gently between his palms. She closed her eyes as his lips met hers in a tender kiss. Reaching for him, she clutched the lapels of his jacket with both hands. The kiss morphed into something more urgent. A need to be closer zipped through her. She savored the moment. This time she had no regrets. Scout yipped softly and pushed his body between their legs. Laughter rumbled in Heath's chest, and he pulled away slightly but leaned his forehead to hers.

"I want to be everything that you and Molly Jo need."

She slid her arms up his shoulders and laced her fingers behind his neck. "You're already the man that I need."

His brow furrowed. "Even if I'm not well?"

Oh, he was so tenderhearted. She brushed another kiss across his lips. "No one is promised an easy life. Let's take things one day at a time, Donovan."

He pulled her against him, wrapping his strong arms around her. She nestled her head against his chest. When she'd met him last July, she'd been a grieving, pregnant widow. A scared single woman who'd taken a leap of faith and moved to this island alone. Then she'd weathered a terrifying disaster, brought Molly Jo into the world and fallen deeply in love with this incredible man. God had brought her out of the depths of her sorrow and led her into an amazing fresh start. Just like she'd always hoped He would.

Epilogue

Eighteen months later

The June sun sparkled on the blue-green water off the coast of Hearts Bay. From their vantage point in a grassy meadow near the Mount Larsen trail, Lexi was certain she could see for miles.

But it was her handsome husband reclining on the striped picnic blanket beside her that offered the best view. Propped on one elbow, he leaned over and gave her a sweet kiss.

"Great picnic, sweetheart." Heath's eyes swept over her in a way that still launched a gazillion butterflies loose in her tummy. "This is the perfect lunch date."

"Agreed." She pressed her palm to his clean-shaven cheek. Today she'd hired a babysitter for Molly Jo and told Heath she wanted more pictures from the Mount Larsen trailhead. Always eager to spend time outdoors, Heath had happily loaded Scout and Lexi's camera bag in the car. She'd packed a picnic and discreetly tucked the small wrapped box in beside their chicken salad sandwiches, potato chips, grapes and chocolate chip cookies. Taking their time eating lunch was a luxury these days. As a spunky toddler, Molly Jo made mealtime a challenge. Scout dozed beside them on their picnic blanket. The only thing that would make the afternoon even better was sharing her incredible news with Heath.

"I hope you're not bummed that we skipped the hike. I do have a surprise for you, though." She pulled the gift from the bag of picnic supplies.

"What's this?" He sat up and examined the rectangular box.

"I told you. A surprise." She'd wrapped the container in white paper with blue polka dots and added a festive curly blue-and-white ribbon.

Eyes gleaming with amusement, he glanced between her and the gift.

"I didn't realize we were exchanging gifts or I would've brought you something. What's the occasion?"

"Open it." Her heart kicked against her ribs. She tunneled her fingers through Scout's curls. He lifted his head and licked her hand, then flopped back down on the blanket.

Heath took his time lifting the tape off one end, before slowly tearing back the paper. Lexi could hardly contain her excitement. She was half tempted to reach over and open it for him.

Finally, he lifted the lid on the box. A square photo of a positive pregnancy test sat on top of a bed of pink-and-white-striped tissue paper.

Heath's mouth dropped open. Birds chirped in the trees nearby. In the distance, a small plane soared over the island. He sat on the blanket, staring at the photo.

His Adam's apple bobbed as he swallowed hard. "Is this...?"

"Heath, I'm pregnant. We're going to have a baby."

He stared at her, his eyes glistening with unshed tears. "Seriously?"

She nodded, blinking back tears of her own.

"I can't believe it," he whispered. He set the box down carefully, then reached for her. She fell against his broad chest. They cried together. Shoulders shaking. Tears sliding down their cheeks.

Scout whined, then sat up, gently nudging them with his big paw.

They pulled back. Lexi laughed through her tears and gave Scout a gentle ear scratch. "It's okay, pal. We're happy."

Heath dragged his fingers across his cheeks. "When did you find out?"

"Early this morning. I took the test and the picture before you woke up." She dried her own tears with the back of her hand. "I used blue wrapping paper and pink tissue paper because it will be a while until we can find out if we're having a girl or a boy."

"It doesn't matter to me." He slid his hand behind her neck, then gently kissed her forehead, the tip of her nose and finally her mouth. She melted into his embrace. Got lost in his kiss. Marveled that this man was hers and their dreams of growing their family were becoming a reality.

When they pulled apart, he looped his arm around her shoulders and reached for the box and photo. "I'm just so happy. This is amazing."

He'd proposed last summer and they'd married quickly in an intimate ceremony on a January night six months ago. Lexi had never envisioned getting married again so quickly, but she and Heath hadn't wanted to wait. Heath's brother, Reid, had been diagnosed with Huntington's not long after they'd come home from their honeymoon, reconfirming their shared belief that life was precious. And often short.

When they'd talked about having children, Lexi had feared Heath would struggle with the knowledge that Huntington's very much had a presence in the lives of his family members. They'd met with the pastor at the church. Asked their small Bible study group as well as their friends and family to pray for them. It had taken a few months to find the right provider for his genetic testing, but they'd finally received the news in early April that Heath wasn't a carrier. He did not have the genetic makeup that would result in Huntington's. And he wouldn't pass it on to his children, either. As much as they were saddened by Reid's diagnosis and what that meant for his future, Heath and Lexi had agreed they didn't want to wait any longer to try to have a baby.

He pressed his palm to Lexi's stomach. "How are you feeling?"

"Not too bad." She covered his hand with her own. "Tired mostly. I'm not that far along yet. Maybe eight or nine weeks."

"How do you think Molly Jo will react?" Heath grinned. "Thrilled or not so much?"

"Thrilled about the idea," Lexi said. "Not so much when the baby lives with us every single day."

His grin broadened. "She's going to be a wonderful big sister."

"The best." She leaned in for another kiss. "You're going to be an incredible father."

"I hope so."

Heath settled back on the blanket and pulled Lexi into his arms. Scout inched closer and rested his snout on her leg. As she lay there on the ground, the sunshine warming her skin, she listened to the comforting thrum of Heath's heartbeat. God had filled their lives with laughter, hope and love. Scout licked her arm. And one amazing Goldendoodle.

* * * * *

If you enjoyed this K-9 Companions book,
be sure to look for A Companion for Christmas
by New York Times *bestselling author*
Lee Tobin McClain, available October 2023,
wherever Love Inspired books are sold!

And pick up these previous books about the
Madden family in Heidi McCahan's
Home to Hearts Bay miniseries:

An Alaskan Secret
The Twins' Alaskan Adventure
His Alaskan Redemption

Dear Reader,

What's the most noteworthy detail about your home state or the community where you currently live? I grew up in Alaska, a state that's well-known for many of its unique attributes. Details about Alaska's history are often on my mind when I sit down to write another book. Hearts Bay and Orca Island are fictional places, but they're inspired by my experiences in Southcentral Alaska. Unfortunately, Alaskans experience numerous earthquakes. My hometown of Valdez was destroyed by an earthquake and a subsequent tsunami on Good Friday in 1964 and impacted by a massive oil spill on Good Friday in 1989. I'm too young to have had first-hand experience with the earthquake; however, I was a middle schooler when the oil spill occurred. We also had plenty of earthquakes and an occasional volcanic eruption that left ash on our yards and vehicles. Those events all provided details that I relied on when I wrote this book, and they inspired the novel's themes of resilience, bravery and helping one another endure challenging circumstances.

As always, the writing process has taught me invaluable lessons. Creating Lexi and Heath's story reminded me of God's promise that He'll never leave or forsake us. My hope is that reading this book will inspire you to reflect on the truths found in God's word and strengthen your relationship with Him.

Thank you for supporting Christian fiction and telling your friends how much you enjoy our books. I'd love to connect with you. You can find me online at Facebook.com/heidimccahan, heidimccahan.com or

Instagram.com/heidimccahan.author. For news about book releases and sales, sign up for my author newsletter at subscribepage.com/heidimccahan-newoptin.

Until next time,
Heidi

COMING NEXT MONTH FROM
Love Inspired

CARING FOR HER AMISH NEIGHBOR
Amish of Prince Edward Island • by Jo Ann Brown

When an accident leaves Juan Kuepfer blind, widow Annalise Overgard and her daughter, who is visually impaired, are the only ones who can help. He needs to learn how to live without his sight, but being around them brings up guilt and grief from the past. Together can they find forgiveness and happiness?

HER HIDDEN AMISH CHILD
Secret Amish Babies • by Leigh Bale

Josiah Brenneman was heartbroken when his betrothed left town without a word. Now Faith Mast is back to sell her aunt's farm—with a *kind* in tow—and Josiah has questions. Why did she leave? Can he trust that she won't run away again? And who is the father of her child?

TO PROTECT HIS BROTHER'S BABY
Sundown Valley • by Linda Goodnight

Pregnant with nowhere to go, Taylor Matheson takes refuge at her late husband's ranch. Then Wilder Littlefield shows up, claiming the ranch is his. He can't evict his brother's widow, so she can stay until the baby arrives—but soon they start to feel like family...

THE COWBOY BARGAIN
Lazy M Ranch • by Tina Radcliffe

When Sam Morgan returns home from a business trip, he's stunned to discover his grandfather has rented the building Sam wanted to his former fiancée, Olivia Moretti. He's determined to keep his distance from the woman who broke his heart, but an Oklahoma twister changes his plans...

A FAMILY TO FOSTER
by Laurel Blount

Single dad Patrick Callahan will do anything to help the foster kids in his care—including saving Hope Center, a local spot for children from disadvantaged backgrounds. When his ex-fiancée, Torey Bryant, is named codirector by her matchmaking mom, it could spell disaster...or a second chance at love.

A FATHER FOR HER BOYS
by Danielle Grandinetti

Juggling a broken foot and guardianship of her nephews, Sofia Russo gladly takes a summer house-sitting gig out in the country. When they arrive, her boys are immediately taken with local landscaper Nathaniel Turner. And she can't help but feel something too. Could he be what they've been missing all along?

LOOK FOR THESE AND OTHER LOVE INSPIRED BOOKS WHEREVER BOOKS ARE SOLD, INCLUDING MOST BOOKSTORES, SUPERMARKETS, DISCOUNT STORES AND DRUGSTORES.

LICNM0723

Get 3 FREE REWARDS!

We'll send you 2 FREE Books plus a FREE Mystery Gift.

FREE
Value Over
$20

Both the **Love Inspired**® and **Love Inspired**® Suspense series feature compelling novels filled with inspirational romance, faith, forgiveness and hope.

YES! Please send me 2 FREE novels from the Love Inspired or Love Inspired Suspense series and my FREE gift (gift is worth about $10 retail). After receiving them, if I don't wish to receive any more books, I can return the shipping statement marked "cancel." If I don't cancel, I will receive 6 brand-new Love Inspired Larger-Print books or Love Inspired Suspense Larger-Print books every month and be billed just $6.49 each in the U.S. or $6.74 each in Canada. That is a savings of at least 16% off the cover price. It's quite a bargain! Shipping and handling is just 50¢ per book in the U.S. and $1.25 per book in Canada.* I understand that accepting the 2 free books and gift places me under no obligation to buy anything. I can always return a shipment and cancel at any time by calling the number below. The free books and gift are mine to keep no matter what I decide.

Choose one: ☐ **Love Inspired Larger-Print** (122/322 BPA GRPA)   ☐ **Love Inspired Suspense Larger-Print** (107/307 BPA GRPA)   ☐ **Or Try Both!** (122/322 & 107/307 BPA GRRP)

Name (please print)

Address   Apt. #

City   State/Province   Zip/Postal Code

Email: Please check this box ☐ if you would like to receive newsletters and promotional emails from Harlequin Enterprises ULC and its affiliates. You can unsubscribe anytime.

Mail to the **Harlequin Reader Service:**
IN U.S.A.: P.O. Box 1341, Buffalo, NY 14240-8531
IN CANADA: P.O. Box 603, Fort Erie, Ontario L2A 5X3

Want to try 2 free books from another series? Call 1-800-873-8635 or visit www.ReaderService.com.

*Terms and prices subject to change without notice. Prices do not include sales taxes, which will be charged (if applicable) based on your state or country of residence. Canadian residents will be charged applicable taxes. Offer not valid in Quebec. This offer is limited to one order per household. Books received may not be as shown. Not valid for current subscribers to the Love Inspired or Love Inspired Suspense series. All orders subject to approval. Credit or debit balances in a customer's account(s) may be offset by any other outstanding balance owed by or to the customer. Please allow 4 to 6 weeks for delivery. Offer available while quantities last.

Your Privacy—Your information is being collected by Harlequin Enterprises ULC, operating as Harlequin Reader Service. For a complete summary of the information we collect, how we use this information and to whom it is disclosed, please visit our privacy notice located at corporate.harlequin.com/privacy-notice. From time to time we may also exchange your personal information with reputable third parties. If you wish to opt out of this sharing of your personal information, please visit readerservice.com/consumerschoice or call 1-800-873-8635. **Notice to California Residents**—Under California law, you have specific rights to control and access your data. For more information on these rights and how to exercise them, visit corporate.harlequin.com/california-privacy.

LIRLIS23

HARLEQUIN
PLUS

Try the best multimedia
subscription service for romance
readers like you!

Read, Watch and Play.

Experience the easiest way to get
the romance content you crave.

Start your **FREE TRIAL** at
<u>www.harlequinplus.com/freetrial</u>.